"Are you planning to stay?" Rob asked.

Kate couldn't read his face, but his voice held a harsh, demanding tone.

She stopped and considered her answer. "I am looking for a job here, something to keep me busy for a few weeks and make me a little money, but I don't plan to stay after Abby's recovered."

This time she could read his expression. Relief, pure and simple.

"Does it matter to you? If I stay or if I leave?"

"Not a bit."

But it did. She didn't need to be a crack investigative reporter to recognize that Rob cared greatly whether she stayed or left.

And he favored her departure, most likely as soon as possible.

Books by Jane Myers Perrine

Love Inspired

The Path to Love
Love's Healing Touch
Deep in the Heart

JANE MYERS PERRINE

grew up in Kansas City, Missouri, has a B.A. from
Kansas State University and has an M.Ed. in Spanish
from the University of Louisville. She has taught
high-school Spanish in five states. She currently
teaches in the beautiful hill country of Texas. Her
husband is minister of a Christian church in central
Texas, where Jane teaches an adult Sunday school
class. Jane was a finalist in the Regency category
of the Golden Heart Awards. Her short pieces have
appeared in the *Houston Chronicle, Woman's World*
magazine and other publications. The Perrines share
their home with two spoiled cats and an arthritic
cocker spaniel. Readers can visit Jane's Web page at
www.janemyersperrine.com.

O LORD, our Lord, how majestic is your name in all the earth! You have set your glory above the heavens. When I consider your heavens, the work of your fingers, the moon and the stars, which you have set in place, what is man that you are mindful of him, the son of man that you care for him? You made him a little lower than the heavenly beings and crowned him with glory and honor. You made him ruler over the works of your hands; you put everything under his feet: O LORD, our Lord, how majestic is your name in all the earth!

—*Psalms* 8:1, 3–6, 9

Many thanks to the Christian adults who gave their time and shared their faith with young people when I was growing up, most especially Wally and Rea Brown, the Russell Smiths, Russ and Betty Huff, Harvey Quenette and Uncle Don.

Also with special love:
Ewart and Prudy Harper Wyle.
George, for years of encouragement and love and for cooking dinner at least twice a week.
Ernest Spiekermann, for his Christian example and for sharing his knowledge of wildflowers of central Texas. Any mistakes are mine, not his.
Jessica Alvarez, the kindest, most talented and patient editor *ever.*

Chapter One

Can't go home again. Can't go home again.
The words repeated in the slap of the car's
worn tires against the highway as Kate Wallace
headed west out of Burnet and into the heart
of the Texas Hill Country.

But here she was, doing exactly that. Going
home. And not a bit happy about it.

She took the curve on Highway 29 too fast.
As the car leaned into the turn, Kate put her
hand on the elderly buff cocker spaniel sleeping
next to her to make sure the dog didn't fall off
the seat.

Why was she in such a hurry? It wasn't as
if the town of Silver Lake would disappear if
she dawdled.

Slowing, she headed north on County Road
144A. Within a few minutes, she was speeding

through rolling hills, past the thick groves of trees and the shimmering green grass that covered central Texas in the spring. Here and there, she spotted patches of bluebonnets, promises of the beauty to come.

Twenty minutes later, she pulled off the highway at the top of the hill that overlooked Silver Lake and kept the engine running.

Scratching her dog Coco's ears, Kate breathed in the spicy scent of cedars as she studied the town spread out below her.

"Kate Wallace," she whispered. "You really are home again." An emotion filled her, an odd mixture of hope and resignation, shame and excitement which made her want to grin and to cry and to flee from here as fast as her old car could take her.

At twenty-one, she'd left Silver Lake with a brand-new degree in journalism and her entire future ahead. Without a backward glance, she'd shaken the dust of small-town Texas off her feet and headed to the big city.

Twelve years later, here she was, back in Silver Lake without her youth and confidence and missing a few other things, as well.

She closed her eyes, trying to replace the view of the small hill-country town with the towering buildings of New York and Houston and the pulsing rhythms of Miami, the cities she'd loved so much. When she opened her eyes the city limits sign—Silver Lake, Population 7,881—stared back at her and the leaves of post oaks rustled in the breeze.

No doubt about it. She was in Mesa County, Texas.

She glanced at her watch. Noon on Saturday. She could sneak into town. With everyone shopping in Austin or Granite Falls, the square would be deserted.

Not that anyone would recognize her now. She was thirty-three and looked every day of it. Her silver-blond hair had darkened over the years and she'd chopped off her long curls six months ago.

Coming home wasn't her choice, but it was the only remaining option. After she'd testified against her boss—a well-known congressman she'd served as press secretary—few choices remained. When her sister Abby's e-mail had arrived three weeks earlier asking Kate to come home and care for her after shoulder surgery, she'd grabbed the opportunity to escape.

She shifted out of Park and stepped on the gas. Within minutes, she passed a new Dollar Merchandise store next to a new H-E-B grocery store.

When a chatting group of people stepped off the curb, Kate returned to reality, slammed on the brakes and stopped inches short of them. *Thank you, Lord,* she whispered, a little surprised at how good that short prayer felt. She couldn't remember the last time she'd said one.

On the sidewalk stood Sara Arroyo, her former best friend. She'd changed, but no one else in town had hair that dark and full and beautiful. Kate should jump from the car and apologize for dropping out of sight. She should tell Sara she was home and they had to get together. But she didn't. Today she wanted to slink back into town. Besides, Sara held the hands of two children. Kate didn't want to interrupt whatever they were doing, an explanation even she recognized as a terrible excuse.

At Lloyd's Auto Repair and Battery Services, she turned left onto Goliad Street. She followed the curve for another block as she drove between rows of towering live oak trees dripping in Spanish moss until she stopped in front of the three-story Victorian house that used to be home.

The house appeared exactly as it had when she took off, the walls still pale yellow with the gingerbread trim painted green, pink and lavender. In the noonday sun, the house, a national historic home, shone like the multi-colored jewel she was.

"That's where I grew up, Coco." The fragile old dog smiled up at her.

Kate hit the trunk latch and got out of the car. After grabbing a couple of worn Louis Vuitton suitcases from the back, she toted them around the passenger side of the car and opened the door. She snapped on Coco's leash and lifted the dog out of the car and onto the grass.

Matching Coco's pace, she ambled to the porch steps where the little dog tried to climb the first step but couldn't lift her arthritic rear leg. The cocker slid down to the stones of the sidewalk, her soft brown eyes focused on Kate, and gave her a "Woof."

"I know, Coco. Old age must be tough." Kate dumped the luggage and leaned down to pick Coco up and place her gently on the porch.

"Why do you carry that dog around?"

Surprised to hear the voice, Kate straightened and saw a girl, probably eight or nine years old, standing inside the front door. She wore pink slacks and a black-and-pink-striped T-shirt. With her hand, the child combed out tangles in her straight brown hair. Who else could she be but her niece? She had Abby's small bones and beautiful features.

"Hello, Brooke. I'm your aunt Kate."

Brooke stared at her.

"This is my dog, Coco."

Coco woofed, not loudly, just as a greeting.

"She's old and has arthritis so she can't get up and down very well."

"That's a really ugly car," she said, then headed upstairs. When she reached the landing, she said, "My mother's at work."

Kate dropped her suitcases on the shiny parquet floor inside. "On Saturday?"

Brooke disappeared without another word.

It wasn't as if Kate were a guest or helpless. She'd grown up here and could find a room for herself. "Stay, Coco," she said as if the little dog would move. She climbed upstairs and looked down the long hall. Three bedrooms and a bath on each side before a right turn into the other wing.

As she contemplated the staircase and the difficulty of carrying Coco up and down, she remembered a bedroom off the kitchen where their housekeepers had stayed years ago. With its private bathroom and proximity to the back door, it would fit her and Coco perfectly.

She found the linen closet and picked out

everything she needed. From below came Coco's soft whimpers. "It's okay," she shouted as she climbed down the steps. Words the elderly and nearly deaf dog couldn't hear but it comforted her to say them. That short phrase was filled with optimism, the hope that everything would be fine, that her sister would welcome her and that Coco would live forever.

When she shoved the door to the small first-floor apartment open, she found a room empty of furniture but with a heavy covering of dust and a few cobwebs. She reached out to touch the wall and felt layers of dust on her fingers. Not up to Abby's usual immaculate standards. That shoulder must really be bothering her to allow dust and cobwebs to accumulate anywhere in her house.

Our house, Kate corrected herself, as her parents had left the house to both daughters.

She went back to the kitchen, dropped the linens on the counter and tried to reorient herself. What she needed was a broom, dustpan, some rags and maybe a chair or two. Where would they be?

For two hours, while Coco slept on a spot of sunshine in the kitchen, Kate swept and mopped, wiped down everything in the small apartment. That completed, she opened the bathroom door and groaned at the state of the tiny place but plowed right in.

Kate had never been much of a housekeeper. At times she wished she'd inherited a smidgen of her mother's compulsive need to clean in her own genetic makeup, never more strongly than now.

"Are you going to stay in here?" Brooke called from the hall outside the bedroom.

"Yes." Kate stood and stretched.

The child glanced around the small area and shook her head.

With one last scrub of the bathroom sink, Kate asked, "Why's your mom at work?"

"Trying to get caught up on stuff."

Exactly like Abby. "Why aren't you out with your friends on a pretty day like today?"

Brooke twisted her hair with a finger. "I don't feel well," she mumbled. "And I like to read. In my room."

Kate didn't pry further. "Is there a bed anywhere I can use?" she said.

Brooke said nothing. Like her mother, Brooke gave less information than anyone needed, but Kate refused to play that game. Arms crossed, she waited.

"There's a shed in the backyard," the child finally said.

Oh, yes, the old shed. Her father had used it for his woodworking shop, his tools mixed companionably with her mother's gardening equipment.

"Thanks." But Brooke was gone.

An odd child, but with Abby for a mother, who wouldn't be? Kate had been surprised that a man as nice as Charles Granger had married Abby, had actually seemed eager to, but he had and this lonely child was the outcome. Where was he now?

Thirty minutes later, with the rooms tidy, Kate headed out back to the shed. Once in the backyard, she paused to remember the glory of her mother's flower beds, imagining the heaps of orange and yellow roses and beds of tulips and daffodils of brightly colored blooms now replaced by thick grass. She wished she'd come back years earlier to see Mom attacking the weeds and fooling with her flowers while Dad built stuff in his workshop. An aching sense of loss rolled over her.

In honor of her mother, maybe she'd plant something while she was here. What else did she have to do except take care of Abby after the surgery? Gardening would allow her time away from Abby before they drove each other crazy.

But she wasn't going to be here long enough.

She'd be leaving in a month, getting on with her life, whatever that meant. She headed to the shed again and shoved the door open to see a jumble of furniture that seemed to have woven itself into an enormous granny knot.

A mattress for a single bed slumped close to the door. She gave a tremendous tug and pulled it out of the building while everything inside shifted with a crash. With a firm grip, she dragged the mattress across the lawn and up the steps. This was like towing a huge piece of overcooked spaghetti, but she finally steered it into the house and dropped it in the kitchen as she gasped for air.

She'd moved the thing this far by herself, and that counted as a big success in a year that hadn't had many. With a few more shoves, she got it into the bedroom. Heady with her victory over the obstinate mattress, she grabbed the sheets and made the bed. That finished, she stepped over Coco and headed to the enormous closet in the front hall.

As a child, she'd taken very literally the scripture advice about where to pray. Back when she was a faithful Christian who really did believe, she'd shut herself in this closet to meditate. Even today the scent of wool and mothballs made her want to fall on her knees.

Shoving away the memory of her former piety and the disappointments that had scuttled her faith, she opened the door and flipped on the light. Yes, the card table and folding chairs were still stored behind the coat rod. She pushed the coats back, picked up a chair and slid the table back to her room. By that time, she realized it was three-thirty and she hadn't eaten lunch yet. A grilled cheese sandwich sounded good and easy.

"What are you making?" Brooke asked.

Kate started when she heard the voice. The child was so quiet, it was like being stalked by a silent, sulky phantom. "A sandwich. Do you want one?"

She shook her head. "Mother doesn't allow me to eat between meals."

"Okay, but I haven't had lunch yet." Why did she feel the need to explain herself to a— "How old are you, Brooke?"

"I'm nine."

Why did Kate feel the need to explain herself to a nine-year-old?

She'd never known exactly when Brooke was born. The baby had suddenly appeared during the dark, silent period after Mom's and Dad's deaths.

Abby hadn't told Kate about the accident

that claimed their lives nearly ten years earlier, either. The first Kate knew they'd died came a month after the fatal automobile crash when the lawyer wrote Kate to explain the terms of their will and her inheritance of half of the estate. Her sister had neither written nor called to tell Kate about their passing or the funeral. She'd never known how to react to such a breach of family…well, conduct by Abby. Fury was the main emotion that filled her until she could finally sort through her grief.

During a telephone conversation almost a year later, Abby mentioned her daughter and, typically, hung up without giving her sister information about her only niece. Kate wasn't about to beg. Pride, another one of her flaws, and a lot of anger kept her from pressing for more details.

All in all, the relationship between the sisters was a case of sibling rivalry gone very bad and very mean. It wasn't *all* Abby's fault, as much as Kate wished she could blame everything on her sister's difficult personality. No, growing up with Miss Mesa County as a sister wouldn't have been easy for anyone. Kate could admit now she'd been a jerk at times. Giddy with her newfound power to attract men, she'd stolen Abby's boyfriend.

Kate hated to admit even now that she'd done anything so petty. Abby had never forgiven her. Nor, she was pretty sure, had the *other* young woman she'd taken a boyfriend from.

"Are you sure you wouldn't like to share half with me?" Kate flopped the sandwich on a plate and turned off the burner.

When Brooke shook her head, Kate poured herself a soft drink and sat down at the table.

Other than playing havoc with personal relationships, her self-centeredness had served Kate pretty well until her world blew up and she didn't have the ability, strength or, really, the desire to deal with it. On top of that, who would have guessed she had a streak of honesty she couldn't ignore? Not her.

When she discovered integrity wasn't a trait greatly respected in her chosen career, she'd slunk back to Silver Lake, to care for the sister who still hated her.

Life sure served up curve balls sometimes.

Looking up to notice Brooke had flitted away again, Kate finished her sandwich, awakened Coco and opened the back door. Even with her bad hip, the dog was able to get down from the porch herself. The problem was getting back up.

While the cocker sniffed around in the yard

and woofed several times, Kate opened the trunk of her car and pulled out the last of her things: her laptop, a box of her favorite books and a flower-covered gift sack, which contained the odds and ends saved over the past twelve years. Everything else—her chrome furniture, the Prada suits and Manolo Blahnik shoes—was in storage in Miami. She grabbed her purse, the now out-of-style Kate Spade bag that had cost *way* too much. She wished she had that money back now. She should have purchased something serviceable and much less expensive at JCPenney as she had her jeans and athletic shoes.

She toted the load into her bedroom. Then she chose a book from the box, grabbed her soft drink and settled in one of the cushioned chairs on the porch. She started to read, leaning her head back against the pillow and relaxing into the lumpy softness.

"Guess that long drive tuckered you out."

Her eyes fluttered open. Birdie Oglesby, school librarian and a pillar of the church, stood on the porch about ten feet from her.

"Hello, Mrs. Oglesby," she said around a big yawn as she stood. "I guess I dozed off."

"Must have needed that nap. I'm just going to put this in the kitchen." The thin little woman with a helmet of tightly permed white hair strode ahead of Kate. She swept into the house like an invader with no resistance in front of her, but an invader with everyone's best interests at heart.

Kate hurried after her. Once in the kitchen, Mrs. Oglesby put a casserole dish on the counter before turning back to Kate, a sincere smile warming her features. "I'm glad you're back, girl. Real glad."

For the first time in months, Kate felt warmth seep through her and smiled back. "Thank you, Mrs. Oglesby. I don't think that's unanimous."

"Most of the town is happy you're back and the others? Well, some people are always negative. Probably no one could win them over, not even you at your most charming."

"But I wasn't always the most pleasant person, Mrs. Oglesby." If Kate had hoped for contradiction here, she didn't get one.

"None of us *always* are," the older woman said. "Now you're back to help your sister in her time of trouble and that wipes out a multitude of shortcomings. Goodness knows, you won't get a thank-you from Abby, but when a family member needed something, you stepped up to the plate."

"Anybody would've…"

"No." Mrs. Oglesby shook her head. "Your sister was supposed to have surgery months ago. No one here would help her, so she finally asked you, and you came." She waved at the dish she'd brought in. "This is a real good chicken spaghetti recipe. The church will bring food for this first week while Abby's recovering. We'll be back next weekend with more."

"Thank you," Kate said as Mrs. Oglesby headed outside.

"We'd like to see you at church tomorrow," the librarian said as the screen door slammed behind her.

Kate had forgotten the generosity of small-town churches. Within the next half hour, fifteen more people brought food—salads, vegetable dishes, casseroles of all kinds, meat, several pies and a cake. As Kate gazed at the number of dishes on the counter, she heard a soft footstep behind her.

"Brooke, I could really use your help putting all this away," Kate said before her niece could disappear. "Why don't you come in and help me." When Brooke continued to rock back and forth in the hall, one foot in front of her, the other behind, Kate added, "I don't even know where the aluminum foil is."

With dragging steps, Brooke entered the kitchen, opened a drawer and waved her hand at the contents.

"Okay, you and I have to decide what we'll eat right away and what to freeze." Kate began to wrap a pie. "What would you like for dinner tonight?"

Brooke pointed at the brisket and several other dishes. "And Miss Betsy's red velvet cake," she said with a bit of animation in her voice. Obviously the cake had power if it could elicit a positive response from Brooke.

"What time will your mother get home?" Kate asked after they finished wrapping and freezing the rest of the food. The question was answered by the sound of the front door opening and banging shut. Footsteps echoed across the hall and Abby came into the kitchen. No smile crossed her sister's still lovely features, no light brightened her dark eyes at the sight of her only sister, but her stiff posture showed that Abby carried a load of tension in her shoulders, neck and jaw.

Kate started to hug Abby because, after all, wasn't that what a person did when she hadn't seen her sister for twelve years? Evidently not. As soon as she touched her sister, Abby stiffened even more and stepped back.

"Hello, Kate," she said as if they'd seen each other only a few hours earlier and that experience had not been particularly pleasant. She moved around Kate and put the mail on the counter. "There's a library notice for you, Brooke. Please take care of it." She handed the card to her daughter and sorted through the other envelopes.

"What's that?" Abby stared as Coco ambled into the room.

"That's my dog, Coco."

When Coco gave a woof, Abby laughed, not a mirthful sound. "You always said you'd have a dog named Coco, but I thought it was going to be a teacup poodle." Abby shook her head. "This poor old thing looks terrible."

"We've been together a long time."

"Looks like it." Abby slipped out of her crepe-soled shoes, picked them up and turned toward the stairway. "I'm going to change. What's for dinner, Brooke?"

"Brisket, Mother."

Abby nodded and walked from the room.

"When do you want to eat?" Kate asked her sister's departing back and scolded herself for allowing Abby's negative attitude to manipulate her again.

"She likes to eat at six, when she's had a chance to rest," Brooke filled the silence.

"Okay, six it is." She gave Brooke the warmest, happiest smile she could manage and was surprised to see a slight curve of the child's mouth. The curve disappeared instantly, but it was a start.

The three joined around the table Kate and Abby's father had built years earlier. "What's your job now?" she asked Abby after they'd passed the dishes and filled their plates.

"Assistant office manager at the bank." Abby cut her meat with her left hand to take the stress off her right side. "Not an easy job. The tellers are young and flighty. I have to put my foot down to get them to work."

"How's your shoulder?" Kate tried another topic.

"I'm having surgery. Rotator cuff. That should tell you." She moved the joint a little and grimaced. "I wouldn't have asked you if things had been fine or if there'd been anyone else."

"I know. I'm glad I can be here. How did you hurt it?"

"I fell." Abby took a few more bites of dinner. "I have to be at the hospital at seven Monday morning."

"All right." They ate in silence until Kate

asked her niece, "Brooke, do you have plans for the summer?"

Brooke blinked as if surprised to be included in the conversation. "Swimming and reading. And I'm going to Waco to visit my father in August."

Having all her efforts at conversation die, Kate gave up. They finished dinner in a thick, uncomfortable silence.

As if they had practiced this routine often, Abby stood and wordlessly left the kitchen and Brooke cleared the table. Before the child could start loading the dishwasher, Coco danced as much as her arthritic hips allowed toward her.

"What's wrong with your dog?" Brooke asked.

"She likes to help do the dishes."

"She does?" A frown wrinkled Brooke's forehead. "How can a dog help?"

"Cleaning up. She hopes a scrap will fall or perhaps someone will put a plate on the floor for her to lick."

Brooke glanced at her aunt. "You actually give her the plate to lick? Mother would kill me if I did that."

"You don't have to, Brooke. That's just what she hopes." Kate picked up a wet sponge and pretended all her attention was on wiping the table, but she could see Brooke select a piece of fat from her plate and toss it to Coco. The dog caught it and smiled. Brooke smiled, really smiled, back at Coco before she became all business and loaded the dishwasher.

"Thanks for cleaning up," Kate said a few minutes later as she dried her hands.

Brooke studied her as if Kate spoke an unknown language. "You're welcome."

"Where are you sleeping?" Abby marched into the kitchen, anger filling her voice. "Why didn't you take the room Brooke got ready for you?"

"Which one was that?" Kate glanced at Brooke. A look of pure panic crossed the child's face. Quickly Kate added, "I decided to sleep downstairs because it would be easier for Coco to get around."

Abby glared at the cocker. "You chose your bedroom based on where your dog would be comfortable?" Hands on her hips, she shook her head. "If that don't beat all."

Abby turned and strode to the small apartment, threw the door open and surveyed the inside. "There's no bed in here, just a mattress on the floor." She whirled to glower at Kate. "I'm not going to have this town say I made my own sister sleep on the floor. I'll call someone to get a bed frame in here."

As Abby stomped away, Kate called after her again, "That was my decision, Abby. You aren't *making* me sleep on…" She stopped as it became obvious her sister didn't want to hear the words.

"Thank you," Brooke whispered.

Kate leaned against the counter to study her niece. "For what?"

"For not telling her I didn't show you that room."

"Why didn't you?"

Brooke fiddled with her hair. "She didn't want you here. Mother…well, Mother always gets upset whenever someone talks about you. I don't like it when she's upset."

"No, I imagine…" Kate stopped her words. She shouldn't agree with Brooke about how difficult Abby could be. "I imagine she loves you very much."

Brooke stared at her as if Kate had come from an alien world. "Oh, sure." She folded the dishcloth and hung it from the sink divider.

She watched her niece, her only niece and one of her two living relatives, leave the room. Was she Abby all over again?

Kate sighed. Why did she care? She wasn't going to be here long enough to connect with

Brooke. She couldn't change anything in a few weeks, but the girl's unhappiness pulled at Kate's heart.

Only a few minutes later, the front doorbell rang. She glanced down. Her shorts had smudges from her earlier cleaning. She'd put on a fresh shirt for dinner, but it had a spot of barbecue sauce on the front from wrapping the brisket. She was barefoot, wore no makeup and guessed her hair stood up in spikes. Why did she care? No one was coming to see her, but because it might be someone with food, she'd better hurry. As she moved toward the entry, Brooke opened the door.

"Hey, Brooke," a man said. "Your mother called. Said she had some furniture she needed moved."

At the sound of that voice, Kate walked backward into the kitchen, almost tripping over Coco. She considered hiding in her room even though she knew the idea was cowardly. Besides, it wouldn't do a bit of good. She suspected that was exactly where the furniture would be going.

In a panic, she glanced around again, searching for a way, any way, to escape.

The voice belonged to Rob Chambers. The one person in Silver Lake she'd hoped never to see again.

Chapter Two

Because the idea of escape seemed cowardly, Kate lifted her head and walked across the wide entry hall, her bare feet pattering on the hardwood floors.

Rob hadn't changed much. His hair was still dark brown with a wave. Years ago, he'd worn a buzz so he didn't have to mess with it. Now it was longer and brushed back in a great haircut.

When he heard her footsteps, Rob turned away from Brooke to watch her. His eyes were still that odd shade of deep blue. Well, of course they were. He had a slight dark shadow across his jaw which made him even more attractive, older and more masculine than the younger Rob had been.

Even now, he was trim, but he carried more

weight than he had at twenty-two, most of it in broad shoulders and a muscular chest. He still wore what had always been his favorite clothing as a teenager: a pair of faded jeans and a T-shirt. And he had the same smile, the one that had always made her want to smile back at him. She couldn't help but grin.

And she also couldn't help but notice that his smile didn't reach his eyes.

"Kate, great to see you. I heard you were back home." Completely at ease, he reached out, put an arm around her shoulder and gave a quick squeeze before he stepped back.

"The prodigal returns," she said. "Can't hide news like that in a small town." They studied each other for a few seconds before Kate asked, "What are you doing now?" He'd always wanted to be an architect, had gone to Texas A&M for that reason while she went to the University of Texas.

"I have my own architectural office in part of my house. We design houses and offices and other structures in about a fifty-mile radius."

"That's terrific, Rob."

"You two know each other?" Brooke glanced back and forth between Rob and Kate. "Well, of course you do. Everyone here knows everyone else."

"We went to high school together," Kate said.

So far, this first meeting with her former fiancé was going better than she'd expected. All these years she'd carried a burden of guilt because she'd thought she'd broken Rob's heart, ruined his life. He didn't appear damaged, not a bit. He'd survived the departure of Kate Wallace quite well.

The old Kate would have been angry to be so easily forgotten. The Kate she'd become was glad Rob could greet her with a smile and an almost hug. Just because her life was in shambles was no reason to hope his was, too.

"In fact, we nearly got married before Kate left town," Rob added.

Brooke's mouth dropped open. "Really?"

"Yes, really." Kate nodded at Brooke before she turned her attention to Rob. "How is Junie?" she asked about Rob's wife.

Brooke and Rob looked at her for a few seconds, then at each other and finally back at Kate again.

"Junie died two years ago," he said. "Cancer."

"Oh, Rob, I didn't know." Kate put her hands to her mouth and shook her head in disbelief. "She was so young." Only five years younger than Kate. Junie'd had the most beautiful red curls and was always filled with life and joy. When Kate heard through one of Abby's infrequent letters that Junie and Rob had gotten married, she'd thought their home must be the happiest place in the world.

"I can't believe it." She shook her head. "I'm sorry."

"Thanks." Rob didn't meet her eyes.

Kate expected him to drop his head and study his athletic shoes, the move she remembered so well. Rob had always done that when he was uncomfortable or didn't want to discuss something.

But that didn't happen. Instead his jaw clenched, his eyes narrowed and he lifted his head to glare over everyone's head.

He'd changed. For a moment, she'd wanted to see the young man she recognized who'd been so courteous and kind. But he'd vanished and a man filled with rage had taken his place.

Almost immediately, he wiped the expression of anger from his face and, as if that reaction hadn't taken place, said to Brooke, "Show me what needs to be moved."

"I put a mattress in my room to sleep on." Kate waved toward the room. "I'm not going to be here very long, so I don't really need much furniture."

"You're not planning to stay around?" Rob

asked. "Everyone's speculating, wondering if you're back for good."

"I'm leaving after Abby recovers from surgery. The reason *you're* here is that Abby thinks I need a bed frame." She shrugged. "I'm okay with only a mattress, but my sister seems to think the neighbors will talk if I don't have a complete bed."

"How would the neighbors know?" Brooke asked.

Kate didn't answer. She'd stopped trying to figure out Abby years ago.

"Well, if it makes Abby happy…" Rob said. "Someone show me the way."

"I think there's a frame upstairs," Brooke said.

"If you'll get that, I'll clear a place for it," Kate volunteered.

Rob started up the steps after her niece, then stopped on the landing to ask, "What size?"

"Single. Grab the easiest one to get to."

"I plan to."

She went back to the bedroom and shoved the sparse furnishings toward one side so Rob could set up the bed. She'd just leaned the mattress against the wall when she heard the sound of scraping across the kitchen floor. "In here," she called.

Rob and Brooke moved gingerly around the

corner, each holding sections of the metal bed frame.

"I'm sorry. I should've helped you."

"There isn't room for anyone else," Rob said as he leaned the metal rails against the wall. "Fortunately this won't be hard to put together." He wiped a little perspiration from his forehead. "Do you want a headboard?"

"Do I need one? Will the frame hold the mattress without it?" When he nodded, she said, "This is fine."

The three worked in the small space, running into each other as they joined rails and turned knobs until the rectangle came together.

"We'll need to get a box spring to hold the mattress," Rob said. All three went upstairs, found what they needed and shoved it down the stairs and into the bedroom.

Not that it was as easy as it sounded. They'd had to move several chairs and a bag of pillows to drag the springs from the room. When Rob and Kate pushed it down the hall, they nearly impaled Brooke against the wall.

The laughter that followed caused Abby to look into the hall and glare at them. "I'm trying to rest." She slammed the door shut.

The movers bit their lips and guided the

springs down the staircase, barely missing Coco, who waited for them at the bottom of the steps. Once in the bedroom, they all fell on the floor and laughed until Brooke jumped to her feet and ran from the room.

"What's the matter with her?" Rob asked as he stood and held his hand out to help Kate to her feet.

"I think she's embarrassed she was having so much fun."

He lifted an eyebrow.

"I know. It doesn't make sense." She shook her head. "You know I never understood my sister. Now I find her daughter nearly as baffling."

In no time, they shoved the springs on the frame and placed the mattress on top.

As they turned to congratulate each other on the accomplishment, their eyes met and the years fell away. During that moment, Kate didn't feel like the young woman who had the world before her and had traded Rob for that dream. No, for just a second, she felt like the girl he'd taken to the prom, like the girl who'd loved him so much, like the girl who'd always planned to come back to Silver Lake and marry Rob.

But she never had, and she was no longer

that girl. And Rob had married someone else and been very happy.

"Daddy, Daddy." A little girl's voice came from the porch outside the kitchen door.

Immediately Rob stepped back and the fragile connection vanished.

"Yes, kitten?" He turned toward the door as a tornado with short red curls wearing pink overalls rushed inside and threw herself at Rob's knees. Laughing, he picked the child up. "This is my daughter, Lora," he said, his voice full of love and pride. "She had a birthday last month and is three years old."

"Three." Lora hesitated for a few seconds before holding up the correct number of fingers.

"Oh, Rob, she's darling." Kate started to reach her arms out to take the child, then stopped. Where had that reaction come from? She was not good with children, not a bit, and hadn't had the slightest desire to pick one up for years. She stepped back a little and said, "She looks like her mother."

He nodded as he nuzzled Lora's hair.

"Puppy, Daddy. Puppy." Lora wiggled in her father's arms to get down as Coco ambled from the bedroom and gave a soft woof.

"She's a very gentle dog." Kate moved toward the cocker and crouched next to her.

Rob placed his daughter on the floor and held her hand as the child pulled him toward Coco. Once there, she patted the dog on the head. Coco smiled up at Lora, who fell to her knees and began to scratch the dog behind the ears.

"Daddy, I want a puppy."

Rob shook his head in frustration. "Kitten, we've talked about this before. When you're older and can help take care of a pet, we'll find you one."

"Daddy, puppy likes me."

"Her name is Coco," Kate said.

"I like Coco." Lora smiled and her blue eyes danced with excitement.

"Don't let my daughter take you in. She can charm anyone to get exactly what she wants." But Rob's gaze at his daughter was soft and filled with love. "Obviously she wants a puppy now."

"You can visit Coco whenever you want, Lora."

But the child was busy scratching Coco's fluffy tummy. Rob and Kate watched the scene until a knock sounded on the screen door.

"Rob, I'm sorry." An older woman with gray

hair and Rob's smile stood outside. "She got away from me."

"Come on in, Mrs. Chambers." Kate welcomed her as she opened the door. "How nice to see you."

"Hello." Rob's mother nodded without making eye contact.

As had been her habit when she and Rob were dating, Kate reached out to hug Mrs. Chambers. When the older woman stiffened, Kate dropped her arms to her sides.

"Heard you were back in town." Mrs. Chambers stared icily at Kate, then stepped away from her to talk to her son. "Rob, your daughter and I started toward the park, but Lora knew you were in here and took off."

"She has a mind of her own," Rob said.

"And you spoil her terribly." Mrs. Chambers shook her head before she smiled. "It's hard not to."

"Kitten, I came here to help Miss Abby." He bent his knees to speak to the child at eye level. "Why don't you stay on the porch with Grandma. When I finish, we'll get some ice cream."

"Promise, Daddy?" She patted his cheek.

"I promise." Rob kissed the small hand and stood, watching his daughter skip out to the porch holding his mother's hand. "And mind your grandmother," he called after them. "As if that's going to make any difference," he mumbled.

"Rob, go ahead." Kate glanced at him, but his eyes followed his daughter. "We're done. Thanks for the help."

She put her hand on his arm, casually, like a friend. In an instant, Kate remembered how she'd felt for Rob years earlier. Odd that sensation remained after so long. Or maybe it was a reaction to this new and very attractive Rob.

"Do you want to join us for ice cream?" Rob's face showed not one bit of enthusiasm for her presence.

As she studied his square jaw and broad shoulders, she realized this wasn't the Rob who'd taken her to the prom. This was the young man she'd left behind. No matter what he said, his expression told her that he didn't want her to join them. Not at all.

"Thanks. I'm tired. Long drive." She yawned. "Maybe another time."

He turned toward the door.

"Your daughter is a doll."

"Yes, she is." He looked back at Kate, his eyes gentle with a father's love. "She's the joy of my life."

* * *

That night Kate tossed and turned for hours. The mattress had a slightly musty smell and several odd lumps. As soon as she thought she'd found a comfortable position, she'd move a fraction of an inch and hit another bump.

At the end of the bed, Coco snored, the soft snuffles of an elderly dog. In the city, covered by the noise of traffic, the snores had never bothered her. Here in the quiet of the country, even the tiniest sound kept her awake.

But it wasn't the mattress or Coco's snores or the sound of the wind and the drone of insects outside her window that wouldn't let Kate sleep. What ate at her and kept her awake was being home and not knowing how and where she fit or even if she did belong, here or anywhere else.

The problem was wondering what the future held for a woman who'd lost any hope of a reference for a new job in her field when she'd testified against her boss.

What kept her awake was the awareness that back when she grew up in Silver Lake, she'd known exactly what she wanted and had the confidence to go after it. Now she no longer possessed either that knowledge or assurance.

All of that kept her awake.

* * *

Kate woke up at seven-thirty the next morning. Sunday morning. The house was quiet. The silence shouldn't have surprised her. The commotion she remembered from years earlier existed only in her memory and in Abby's.

When Dad was alive, by this time on a Sunday morning, he'd been up for an hour fixing breakfast. The aroma of hickory-smoked bacon and coffee would have wafted from the kitchen while Mom dashed around waking her daughters and trying to keep them alert long enough to get out of bed and come down for breakfast.

If nothing else reminded her that her parents were no longer alive, the quiet house and the complete lack of tantalizing scents coming from the kitchen would have convinced her. The sense of loss hit her hard. For a moment, she felt the absence of her mother and father so strongly she had to hold back the tears.

How she wished she could go back all those years and wake up to see them smiling at each other and working together. Mom would be listening as Dad explained for the thousandth time how to cook bacon so it was crisp and the advantages of using newspaper to scour out the old black iron skillet.

She should have come home years ago.

Tossing the covers back and wondering why she was so wide-awake after tossing and turning half the night, Kate stood, slipped on her slippers and shrugged into a robe.

With Coco behind her, she wandered into the kitchen.

"What are you doing up so early?"

She jumped when she heard Brooke's voice. Her niece had sneaked up on her again. "I thought I'd go to church with you this morning," Kate said.

Why had she said that? She hadn't been to church for years and hadn't even considered it until the words emerged from her mouth. Maybe the fact was that she didn't go to church in New York or Houston or Miami but she did in Silver Lake. Well, attending the service probably wouldn't hurt her. Besides, it would be nice to see the people who'd been so nice, who'd brought food, and to accept Mrs. Oglesby's invitation.

"We don't go to church," Brooke said, her voice muffled as she stuck her head in the refrigerator.

When Brooke straightened and pulled out a jar of jelly, Kate asked, "You don't go to church? We always went to church when I lived here."

Brooke could have said, "You haven't lived here for a long time," but she didn't. Instead she twisted the tie off a loaf of bread, took out a slice, put it in the toaster and pushed the lever down. Any observer would've thought the silver surface covered the most fascinating invention in the universe from the way the child contemplated it.

"Well," Kate asked the back of Brooke's head, "do you want to come with me?"

Brooke turned and stared at her aunt with those somber eyes, looking older and sadder than any nine-year-old should be. Of course, Kate hadn't been acquainted with many nine-year-olds since she helped with the junior fellowship at church when she was in high school. None of those kids had ever gazed at her like this, their expression full of sorrow.

"Okay," Brooke mumbled before the toast popped up and she grabbed it.

Still a little surprised by her decision to go to church, Kate decided to skip Sunday school and eat a leisurely breakfast, occasionally dropping a tidbit for Coco. As she read the paper, she noticed that Brooke would glance at her aunt, then surreptitiously drop a small piece of toast to the dog.

By ten-thirty, Kate had showered and dressed

in a nice pair of taupe slacks and an ecru silk shirt she hoped would be acceptable for church in Silver Lake. She hadn't brought a dress with her—she hadn't planned to go anyplace that needed one.

By ten-thirty, she was also running late. She left Coco sleeping on her bed, grabbed her purse and ran outside to the front porch where Brooke waited. "Do you want to walk or ride?"

Brooke didn't say a word, just looked in the direction of Kate's car with a raised eyebrow. The silent response was obvious. She wouldn't be caught dead in that thing.

"Okay, let's walk."

It wasn't far. As children, they'd made the trip in less than five minutes, but today Kate wore sandals with two-inch heels and was accompanied by a less than enthusiastic companion. Even with all that, they arrived five minutes before the service started.

With each step, she could see more of Bethany Church. She'd always thought it was a lovely building and had compared it favorably to every church she attended before she stopped going completely five years earlier.

At the end of the first block, the tall wooden cross on top of a roof shingled with black slate punched through the treetops. She kept her eye on it and the few cars on the street as she encouraged Brooke to keep up with her.

When they crossed the street Kate saw a woman coming toward them, a woman who glowered at Kate as if she were the lowest form of life in the universe.

Kate forced herself to smile into the frown of Sandra Dolinski. "Hello, Sandra. How are you?"

Sandra didn't answer, only stared a few more seconds before she turned and strode away as Kate watched.

Although yearning to say something to that straight, judgmental back, Kate bit her lip. She'd hoped her long absence had washed away any resentment about how high and mighty Kate Wallace had been back then.

Guess not.

"Who was that?" Brooke asked. "Why was she so mean?"

"I wasn't always nice when I was in high school." Kate headed toward the church again, not wanting to explain that Sandra's was one of the boyfriends she'd stolen. She had to apologize to her someday.

After the confrontation with Sandra, Kate really did worry about her reception at church. Would there be others there who remembered the old, petty, conceited Kate? Who would like to get back at her?

She pushed the thoughts aside and kept walking. She could hardly turn around and go back home now, not when she'd talked Brooke into coming, not when it meant giving in to Sandra's anger.

When they were half a block from the church, the windows of the youth and children's Sunday school department peeked through the leaves. Cars turned off the street and into the parking lots or pulled up to park against the curb.

Next, the beautiful stained-glass window of Jesus praying in the garden appeared through a break in the branches.

Finally, as they turned onto the broad sidewalk in the front of the building, she saw the strength and beauty of the church. Built of pale gray limestone quarried from the hills in the area, it looked as if it would stand for eternity. As she entered the front doors, she was struck by a deep yearning for the faith that used to sustain her. Even stronger was regret that she'd lost the assurance of that faith over the past few years in the shuffle of her life, under the layers of what she'd thought was more important.

They were late enough that most of the congregation had settled in the sanctuary except the few who straggled in from the street with her. Through the open doors between the sanctuary and the greeting area, she heard the organist playing the prelude and a low buzz of conversation. No one had ever learned that the prelude was supposed to be a time of quiet meditation, not a meet-and-greet session. Another thing that hadn't changed in Silver Lake over the years.

She took three more steps until she stood barely inside the sanctuary. A woman she didn't know handed her an order of worship and Brooke tugged at her hand to pull her down the aisle. Oddly the child headed toward an empty pew while Kate, afraid there were more like Sandra Dolinski inside, wanted to whirl around and run.

Who was she fooling by coming to church after so many years? Certainly not God.

Why was she here? Although she knew most of the people inside would welcome her, she feared the judgment and gossip that might greet her after her time away.

Many years earlier she would have prayed for strength from God, but they weren't on that good of terms anymore. All her fault, she knew.

The irony that today she needed strength from God before entering His house was not lost on her.

"Come on, Aunt Kate," Brooke whispered loudly enough for everyone inside to turn around and watch them.

She took a deep breath and followed Brooke toward a pew a few rows behind Rob and his mother and across from Mrs. Oglesby.

"Oh, dear Lord," she whispered. "What am I doing here?" And yet, as the service began, the music filled and lifted her; the beauty and truth of the scripture inspired her; and the sermon both challenged and comforted her.

After the service, people gathered around her, people who greeted her and were glad to see her. A lovely surprise.

"So nice to have you home," her grade-school principal said. "We're proud how you stood up against that crooked congressman."

"Takes a lot of courage to do that," Mrs. Watkins, her high school journalism teacher said, and patted her on the shoulder. "Good job."

Mrs. Watkins had what was called "big Texas hair." So blond it was almost white, it puffed from her head like a giant dandelion-gone-to-seed, but a very nicely colored and well-coiffed dandelion-gone-to-seed. Like other women with "big Texas hair" she had flawless makeup and her fingers, ears and neck—every square inch possible—glittered with jewelry.

"Thank you." She'd always loved this teacher. Mrs. Watkins's enthusiasm and knowledge had been her motivation for getting a degree in journalism.

Grabbing Kate's hand with her beautifully kept fingers, Mrs. Watkins said, "If you're looking for something to keep you busy while you're here, I've got a part-time job at the *Sentinel*. I'm editor there now."

"You are? Congratulations." But before she could tell her she was not interested in a job, people surrounded them, chatting.

After more greetings and pats on the back, Kate knew why she was in this place, in Bethany Church.

"Thank you, God," she whispered as she left with Brooke. "Thank you for bringing me home." Even if the methods God used seemed circumspect and the road home bumpy, she was grateful. It felt good to be here, to be welcome. To belong.

Now all she had to do was to persuade

Sandra Dolinski and her sister to forgive and accept her, too.

Without a lot of guidance and grace from God, there was little chance of that.

Chapter Three

Kate hated hospitals.

Not that she'd ever spent the night in one. She'd spent only a few minutes several times cheering up sick friends.

And not that everyone else in the world loved hospitals. Other than the staff, probably no one even liked hospitals. She guessed every patient tucked into pristine cubicles wished they were someplace else.

In the waiting room, Kate leaned back in a metal chair with a thin cushion upholstered in sticky plastic. Yawning, she shifted in an attempt to find a comfortable place, but a comfortable position didn't exist.

She'd gotten up at five-thirty that morning to dress and grab a cup of coffee before she awakened Brooke. While Brooke ate, Kate took Coco outside, found a tree with plenty of shade and settled the dog there with a bowl of water and a blanket.

That accomplished, Kate dashed into the house and glanced at the clock. It had been almost six-fifteen. The doctor wanted Abby at the hospital by seven.

Now sitting in the surgery waiting room while Abby was being prepped, Kate began a gradual collapse. She was not a morning person—5:00 a.m. was the earliest she had been up for years, and certainly not since she was a hot new reporter for the morning report on a Houston television station.

As she began to doze, through the fog she heard the approach of footsteps. When they stopped in front of her, she opened her right eye a slit to see Reverend Moreno. With a start, she jumped to her feet and reached out her hand. "Good morning, Reverend. How nice to see you."

He took her hand and shook it. "And a surprise I believe from your expression." His English held a slight Spanish accent and an interesting rhythm, almost like a song. "I come to the hospital anytime a member of the congregation is admitted." He let go of her hand. "Please sit down."

When she did, he sat next to her.

"Is Abby still a member of the church?" she asked. "From what Brooke said, they don't attend regularly."

"No, they don't, but they are members and may return to us." He smiled. "After all, we must never give up on the leading of the Holy Spirit."

Kate nodded and struggled not to yawn.

"You must be tired."

"I've had a busy few days, and I don't like getting up early."

"And yet you came to church yesterday. Everyone was glad to see you." He nodded in a very pastoral manner. "I hope you'll come again." Reverend Moreno stood. "Do you want to come with me while I pray with your sister?"

"No, but thank you."

As the minister headed toward preop, Kate wondered why she hadn't gone with him. Praying with her sister might open something up between them. That would be good. However, it could also toss up another wall between them if Abby felt Kate had intruded on her private space. Hard to guess Abby's reaction but more likely the latter.

After several cups of coffee, a couple of

walks around the small hospital, reading every page of the Austin newspaper and an ancient *People* magazine and watching the morning news, a woman dressed in surgical scrubs emerged from the operating suite.

"Miss Wallace?" she called after glancing down at a chart she held.

Kate stood. "I'm Kate Wallace."

"I'm Dr. Norris. Your sister did fine. The operation should resolve the problem."

"Good."

"She's in recovery now. If you'd like to go to room…" The doctor consulted the chart. "Five-eleven. She'll be there in a short time."

"Five-eleven," she repeated. "Thank you."

Leaving the waiting room, Kate headed toward the patient wing. Once she found the room, she settled into the reclining chair and, again, closed her eyes.

Abby would be in the hospital for a day or two, then they'd release her to Kate's care for a convalescence lasting four to six weeks.

If they both survived that long.

There she went again, always thinking about herself. The convalescence would be harder on Abby than on her. Her sister would be in pain. Even worse, she'd have to accept the help from—in fact be completely dependent on—

Kate, the sister she'd never particularly liked. Because the entire situation would be difficult for Abby, Kate should—would—have to be nice. Try to be nice. Force herself to be nice.

She'd always worked with the public and, over the years, had developed a method of dealing with difficult, demanding people. But this was her sister, the woman who knew every one of Kate's hot buttons and loved to push them.

However, this older Kate Wallace knew how to deflect those barbs better than she had as a child. Besides, she really wanted to get along with her sister.

How far would good intentions take her? She closed her eyes and sighed. The four-to-six week thing began to sound longer and longer.

"Excuse me." An orderly entered. "We need you to leave until we have the patient settled."

After she stood and left the room, two orderlies wheeled in a gurney with Abby on it and a nurse followed.

In the hall, Kate paced up and down for a few minutes before she saw Rob emerging from the gift shop with a bouquet of yellow roses.

For a moment, she stopped and watched

him, the determined gait, broad shoulders covered by a blue knit shirt and the confident lift of his head. Wow. Rob was gorgeous. A real man, he'd draw the interest of any woman in Houston or Miami. Here his good looks and self-assurance filled the narrow corridor with potent and very masculine appeal.

"How's the patient?" he asked before he glanced at a note in his hand. "She's in room five-eleven?"

As she fell in step beside him, Kate forced her senses from her sudden and unwelcome interest in Rob and her brain back to her sister's health. "The doctor says she's doing well."

"But?" He glanced at the closed door then back at Kate.

"I don't know. I haven't seen her. She just got out of recovery and they're getting her settled." In a flash, the enormity of what lay ahead, weeks of taking care of Abby, overwhelmed her. She leaned on the wall and took a deep breath.

"Worried?"

She glanced into eyes that showed concern. "I thought I knew what I was getting into, but, Rob, I've never been a good nurse and Abby and I've never gotten along. What if I can't do this?"

"Hey, you'll be fine." He studied her face.

"I know how determined you can be. Once you start something, you don't give up."

She attempted a smile. "That's not always true."

"Often enough," he added in a voice filled with certainty. "Kate, you can."

"I hope so."

He hesitated for a moment before saying, "I saw you in church Sunday. I didn't get to greet you because I had to pick Lora up from children's church."

"I saw you."

"Kate, I don't know if you still pray like you did as a kid." He reached out to touch her arm but it seemed as soon as he realized what he was doing, he dropped his hand. "If you don't think you can handle things, pray about them. There's a source of strength outside of us. You used to know that." His gaze stayed on her face. "I don't know if you do anymore, but you did. He's still there."

"I'm really out of practice."

"'Whisper a prayer in the morning,'" Rob sang softly.

The tune took Kate back years, to church camp and the memory of the voices of two hundred high school kids lifted in song. "'Whisper a prayer at noon,'" she sang back.

"See? You remember."

How could she forget? The song reminded her of a time she believed God answered prayers. Why had God seemed so close, so present in her life when she was young? How had she lost Him? Well, she hadn't so much lost God as misplaced Him beneath priorities that no longer seemed so important.

The door to Abby's room opened. "You can come in," the orderly said as he left.

Rob held out the bouquet. "Do you want to take these in?"

"No, she'd like to see you." She pushed the door open and looked inside. Abby lay on the bed closer to the hall. Her right arm was strapped securely across her chest, which would probably make sleeping difficult.

She was pale. With her eyes closed, Abby's long lashes showed as a dark fringe against her chalky cheeks. Kate moved silently across the few feet that separated the door from the bed. She put her hand on her sister's left shoulder and whispered, "How are you doing?"

Abby's eyes opened a slit at the same time her jaw clenched. "Hurt," she muttered. "What did you think?"

"Did they give you something for pain?"

She closed her eyes and nodded.

"Abby, Rob's here. Would you like to see him?"

Abby nodded again.

After he entered, Rob placed the flowers on the bedside table then moved next to Abby's bed. "How're you doing, slugger?"

Slugger? She couldn't imagine anyone calling Abby that.

"Okay." She sighed. "Groggy."

"I'll keep you in my prayers."

Abby nodded only a moment before her eyes closed.

As they moved toward the door, Kate whispered, "Thanks for coming."

"If I can help you, call."

After Rob left and with Abby sleeping, Kate headed toward the hospital cafeteria. As she ate her salad, she wondered if Rob remembered what else had happened at church camp or if he'd buried those memories, replaced them with newer ones.

But she'd never forget that it was there on the banks of Silver Lake she'd received her first kiss and fallen in love with Rob.

Did he remember that? Probably not, because she'd left him, he'd married Junie and thoughts of their lives together had replaced the earlier ones. Maybe it was Kate who hadn't moved on, who was filled with recollections of their years together.

After lunch, the afternoon turned into a boring few hours as Abby slept. At four, Kate stood. "I'm going home to check on Brooke."

As she walked past the nurses' station, the head nurse said, "Miss Wallace?"

Kate stopped. "Yes?"

"The physical therapist will be here at eight in the morning to get your sister started on a few exercises."

"But she just had surgery."

"It's better to start right away. Can you be here? You'll need to help her with the exercises when she goes home."

"Of course."

A few hours later, after Kate took Brooke to see her mother, they grabbed a pizza. The child devoured her two-thirds and ran off to do homework while Kate again took her glass of tea to the back porch.

Kate leaned back in the chair and studied the sky while Coco patroled the yard. Without the competing light of a city, the stars shone so much more brightly here. She lifted her head to allow the breeze to cool her cheeks, a breeze that carried the fresh scent of lilac bushes and recently mowed grass from the yard across the fence.

From the Dkanys' porch came the sound of a show tune. They'd always joked about whether Trixie or Paul had control of the radio dial. She liked oldies; he preferred country.

Surrounded by the familiar sounds and scents and the chirping of locusts, she was filled with peace. "Thank you, Lord," she whispered, words which caused her to wonder how she'd been able to pray like that, so easily as if she were used to thanking God.

And how could she feel at home and at rest in a place she'd longed to escape nearly half a lifetime ago? She should be bored, but she wasn't. She should long for the excitement of a life of running from one reception to another, from a meeting with this official to an interview with the press corp., but she wasn't. She actually liked sitting alone in the backyard of her childhood home.

Why?

Finding no answers to her questions, she stood and called Coco.

"Come on." She whistled. The cocker woofed then ambled toward her and sat at the edge of the porch, front paw on the step.

As she picked up Coco and put her on the

porch she thought how handy it would be if there were some way Coco could get up on the porch by herself. Maybe some small steps or a lift. As if she could afford either.

Maybe she could put together some steps that would be easier for Coco to climb with rocks and scrap lumber. Rob probably had old wood at a construction site. Although she used to work in the wood shop with her father, putting such a project together was beyond her meager ability now. Besides, how would she get large enough rocks and how could she move them?

No, that wouldn't work, but if she could build a sloping platform or maybe a ramp…

A ramp. Exactly!

After all, she was going to be here at least four more weeks. During that time, Coco needed to be able to get on the porch by herself.

A ramp would work. But who could she find to build it? Did Rob still like to work with his hands or was he too busy with his practice? She hated to ask him, even though he'd told her to call on him. It felt unsettling to be around him because, well, there was that attraction she couldn't deny and didn't want to feel. Being close to him was uncomfortable, which was absolutely absurd. They'd both gone on with their lives successfully.

The whole attraction thing bothered her for many reasons, not the least of which was because she'd just arrived home from a terrible change in her life, an experience which had taught her she couldn't trust anyone, which had left her wounded and friendless. This was not the time to find any man interesting, especially not Rob.

On top of that, she realized her reaction wasn't to Rob as the young man she'd been in love with. No, she saw him as the older, more mature and very different Rob. The whole awareness of Rob as a man made her slightly unbalanced and decidedly confused. She, who had dealt with high-ranking politicians, interviewed senators and governors and faced hostile reporters, was flustered being around Rob, whom she'd known all her life. How foolish was that?

But if she didn't ask Rob, she couldn't think of anyone else. Would someone at the church be able to help? They'd been awfully nice, but building a ramp for a dog would seem foolish to most people.

No, she'd have to continue to pick Coco up and put her on the porch and hope the cocker didn't hurt herself trying to do that herself.

Didn't some company manufacture portable ramps? If they did, she could handle that on her own. Just open it and leave it there while they were in Silver Lake, then fold it up and take it wherever they went.

She'd think about it, but first she'd better get inside and get ready for bed. This had been an early morning. Tomorrow she'd also need to get up early to get Brooke off to school before she headed to the hospital for the PT appointment.

With a yawn, she stretched and turned toward the house. The cocker followed her inside and into Kate's bedroom. Or, as Coco probably considered it, the room she allowed her person to share.

Chapter Four

Bluebonnets covered the hills with a light purple haze, a shade somewhere between blue and lavender, which could seldom be caught in a photo or description. The sight filled Kate with amazing joy to be home.

Kate had started for the hospital a little earlier than necessary so she could catch the shimmer of the last trace of dew as the petals caught the sunlight. Although the wildflowers were not at their glorious peak, in a few more days the flowers would grow thick along the verge of the road and paint every inch of pasture with their vibrant beauty.

For a moment she pulled off the road to revel at the colorful scene before she stepped on the gas. Abby wouldn't appreciate her arriving late because she'd been gawking at wildflowers.

After she entered Abby's room ten minutes later, Roger Davis, the physical therapist, explained the process. "The idea of physical therapy is to teach the body that it's okay for the joints to move."

Abby lay flat, arms in the air to accept the cane the physical therapist placed in her hands.

"Don't force the movement." The therapist watched his patient before he turned to Kate and said, "You'll have to make sure she does all six of these exercises five times a day." He passed Kate several pieces of paper stapled together.

"I can do them myself," Abby grumbled.

The expected response. Kate knew her sister wouldn't take kindly to having her younger sister help her. Not in any way.

"You'll also have to help Mrs. Granger with dressing, showering and getting out of bed," Roger said.

"I can handle all of those for myself," Abby repeated.

The therapist turned toward Abby. "Mrs. Granger, if you use that shoulder before it's healed or don't complete the PT, you may need surgery again."

For a moment, Abby shut her eyes. After what looked like an intense internal struggle, she said, "All right," in a voice that expressed grudging acceptance of the therapist's warning.

"For the next exercise, you'll need a pulley attached to a door and a rope with handles." He handed Kate a diagram.

Kate studied the picture. "I'll go to the hardware store and look for these." She put all the information in her purse. "So, four to six weeks for recovery?"

"That's pushing it a little." The therapist picked up his clipboard. "More like six to eight. The injury was more complex than the surgeon expected."

Six to eight? Well, okay. What difference did a few weeks make? Maybe with a few extra days, she'd know where she'd end up after her sister's recovery.

By ten-thirty, Abby had received her physical therapy, prescriptions and discharge orders with a doctor's appointment set for a week later. Over her continued protests, she'd been helped into a wheelchair and pushed by an orderly to the front door while Kate brought her car around.

On the trip home, Abby leaned back against the car seat holding her firmly immobilized right arm. Her clenched lips and pallor showed how much the surgery and the physical therapy had worn her out.

"Doing okay?" Kate asked after stopping at a red light.

Abby nodded.

A few minutes later, she pulled the old car into the driveway, stopped and turned off the ignition. "Well, here we are." Could she say anything more obvious? "Let me help you out of the car." She leaped out her side and ran around to the passenger door, opened it and started to reach in.

How should she do this? She couldn't grab Abby's protected right side but she couldn't reach the left side. "Can you turn in the seat a little?"

Abby glared at Kate. The fact that Kate could see only one eye didn't diminish the power of that hostile expression.

Okay, she's just had surgery. She's bound to be grumpy. Then to her surprise, Kate thought, *Dear Lord, please give us both patience.*

Where were these prayers coming from? Not that she minded, but it was odd. Why was she suddenly praying like she had when she was a religious kid?

"Need any help?" Rob jogged to the car from the backyard. "Thought Abby might need another arm to help her out of your car." He scrutinized the car for a few seconds. "Although I'm not sure what you have really is a car. When I first saw it, I thought someone had left a pile of junk in front of the house."

Feeling no need to defend her pitiful old vehicle, Kate asked, "How did you know we were here?"

"Mrs. Oglesby called me when you drove up."

She glanced across the street at the brown Craftsman home where the Oglesbys lived. "It's May. Why isn't Mrs. Oglesby working? It's too early for summer vacation."

"Time passes, Kate. She retired a few years ago."

"She's sixty-five?" Kate considered that.

"At least," Abby mumbled.

"Since Mr. Oglesby died last year, she spends all her time volunteering and keeping an eye out for the neighbors."

"You know, I never knew how old teachers were. They all look about the same age and seem to go on forever." She shook her head. "When I was gone, I never thought anything changed back here. I guess I fantasized that I'd come back here and everything would be the same."

Ouch. Was that the wrong thing to say. During those years, Rob had finished school, married, had a baby and lost his wife. She needed to watch her tongue.

"How nice of her to call," Kate said in a hasty effort to erase her thoughtless words.

"She saw you drive by with Abby and thought you both needed some help. My office is over there." He waved toward the alley. "The old Perkins house."

"You bought the old Perkins house?"

"Five years ago. My office is in the old side porch and living room. Didn't you see the sign?"

She shook her head. "I haven't done any exploring since I arrived."

"I remodeled the garage. Mom lives there. Makes it nice for Lora to have her grandmother so close."

"If you two can stop reminiscing, I need to rest," Abby interrupted sharply as she attempted to turn in the seat. "In my bedroom, not out here."

"Hold your horses. We'll get you inside," he said.

Odd how Rob could talk to Abby like that. She didn't mind his kidding and almost smiled.

"Here's what we're going to do." Rob moved closer to the front seat and leaned down. "Kate's going to get in on the driver's side and nudge you across the seat. I'm going to grab your good arm and help you stand."

The plan worked. Within a minute, Rob held Abby's left arm to steady her as they walked across the sidewalk and up onto the porch.

After Kate ran ahead and opened the doors, she stood in the front hall and looked around, worried. With Abby moving this slowly and tentatively, how was she going to make it up the steps?

"Those stairs will be hard for you," Kate said as Abby entered on Rob's arm. "Why don't you stay in my room for just a few weeks while you recuperate?"

"Your dog lives there." Although a spasm of pain caused Abby to close her eyes, she kept her voice clear and level. "I'm not going to live with a dog, not for any reason."

"Then sit down and rest until we can get you upstairs." As Abby settled on the closest chair in the living room, Kate said, "You know, Rob and I could move some furniture and make the living room into your bedroom for a few weeks."

"I don't need a bedroom down here." She

sniffed. "Wouldn't be proper to sleep in the parlor. I can make it upstairs." Abby grabbed Rob's arm, pushed herself to her feet and shuffled toward the stairs still leaning against him.

Kate followed. Not that she was much help. The only use she'd be was if Abby slipped and fell. Then she could cushion her sister's fall. Of course, she could put her hands on her sister's back to keep her steady, but Kate knew good and well what Abby's reaction to that would be.

After they entered the bedroom and Abby collapsed onto a love seat, Rob let go of her arm. "I'll leave the two of you alone and let myself out." He headed toward the door. "Let me know if you need anything."

"We need a pulley," Abby said. "For my exercises. Kate has a picture."

"A pulley?" He stopped and turned to face Kate. "Okay. I'll pick you up this afternoon to go to the hardware store, Kate. Bring the picture. We'll get what you need and I'll put it together."

"Rob, you have to work," Kate protested.

"Hey, I can take a break. Mom says I work too hard, anyway."

"But you've…"

"Kate, you forget about small towns. We help each other. Call me when you're able to go." He reached in his pocket and pulled out a card. "This is my cell-phone number."

She nodded.

After he left, Kate walked slowly toward Abby. "I'll help you get into your nightgown."

Abby muttered under her breath but allowed Kate's assistance, happy to climb into bed.

"Lunch?" Kate asked, but Abby was asleep before she could answer.

A loud knock sounded on the kitchen door as Kate prepared a sandwich for herself. Popping a sliver of the sandwich into her mouth, she walked toward the door and opened it.

On the back porch stood Sara Arroyo. A very unhappy Sara Arroyo, her hands on her hips and a glare creasing her brow.

Kate had certainly been on the receiving end of a lot of glares recently.

"All right," Sara demanded. "How long were you going to hide here before you got in touch with me?" She pushed the door farther open, walked past Kate and inside to lean against the counter and continued to glower. Obviously another person not expecting a hug after all these years.

"I wasn't hiding. I went to church Sunday."

Sara nodded. "I heard that. I didn't make it, but your presence was whispered about all over town."

Better to tell the truth. "I didn't call because I thought you'd be mad at me."

"Oh, like not calling is better. And why would I be angry?" She glared as she considered the statement. "Because you didn't get in touch with me for—" she counted on her fingers "—oh, yes, fifteen years?"

"Only twelve," Kate protested, as if that were better.

"Okay," Sara said, "that's easily fixed. Tell me you're sorry and you'll never run off and cut off all communication again."

"I am and I won't." She'd missed Sara and her no-nonsense manner. "I really am sorry. I feel terrible I left without a word and I've been gone all these years and never wrote, never called."

"I would've liked to hear from you, would've loved it if you came back to town and dropped by, but I went on with my life, you know." Sara pulled out a stool and settled on it. "It didn't stop because my best friend bailed out."

"I didn't…"

"Yes, you did. You left us all behind because you wanted to shine in the big world. I understood that. We all did, but I do think an old friend would let me know when she's finally back in town instead of letting me hear it from Sandra."

"I am sorry. Truly." After the second apology, Kate glanced toward the bread and brisket, the beginning of her sandwich. "Do you want lunch? Something to drink?"

She pointed at Kate. "Don't think you're going to bribe me with a sandwich. I'm not as easy to manipulate as Mr. Robbins in junior English, who never gave you detention when you arrived late to class because you apologized so sweetly."

"I wouldn't dream of that."

Sara shook her head and a smile broke through the grimace. "I don't care. I could never stay mad at you for long." She held out her open arms. "Glad to see you. We've got some catching up to do, *chica.*"

Finally someone wanted to hug her. After returning the embrace, Kate took another plate and glass from the cabinet. "What do you use on your sandwich? Mustard? Mayo?"

"Salsa."

"Of course." Sandwiches complete, Kate

got chips out and dumped them into a bowl and filled their glasses with ice. "It's really great to see you, but don't you work? How can you take off to see me?"

"No one dares tell me I can't take off for a few minutes." She poured herself a glass of tea from the pitcher Kate had placed on the counter. "How's your sister doing?"

"We just got home. She's sleeping. Do you want to visit her?"

Sara shivered. "No, thank you. I can only imagine how hard she is to get along with when she's had surgery." She grimaced. "Sorry. Shouldn't have said that about your sister. I admire you for coming home to take care of her."

Kate shrugged. No need to explain the reasons she'd come home hadn't been completely altruistic. She settled in a chair and asked, "So, how long have you and Pete been married? Any kids?"

"Pete and I never got married," she stated matter-of-factly before she took a bite of the sandwich.

"What? But you were planning the wedding when I left. I was going to come back and be maid of honor."

"Didn't you notice I never got in touch with

you about buying a dress or told you the date for the wedding?"

Kate nodded. At the time she'd been so busy and ambitious that she hadn't really noticed it. The years since had passed, and the few times she thought about Silver Lake, she'd assumed Sara and Peter had married.

"What happened?"

She shrugged again. "It didn't work out."

Obviously that subject was closed. Kate switched to another topic. "So where do you work?"

"You don't know, do you? After Peter and I broke up I went to A&M and got a degree. I'm a veterinarian now."

"You're *Dr.* Arroyo?"

As she crunched on a few chips, Sara nodded.

"Well, I'm impressed." Kate held her hand up. "Not surprised but impressed."

"You should be. That was a long, hard road. I came back and worked with Dr. Nichols until he retired a few years ago. He sold me the practice on very good terms. Last year, I hired another vet to give me a hand. I couldn't take care of the animal population of the entire county by myself plus the kids."

"The kids?"

Before Sara could answer, Kate heard a voice calling her name. "Sounds like Abby." She jumped to her feet. "Can you stay a little longer?"

"No." Sara swallowed the rest of her tea then wrapped the remaining sandwich in a napkin. "I've got appointments starting in ten minutes. See you later." When Kate started to walk her to the door, she shooed her away. "Go ahead. I can get out by myself."

"It's about time." Abby frowned when her sister entered the bedroom. "I've been calling forever."

"Sorry. I didn't hear you. Did you have a nice nap?"

"Yes, until I woke up and discovered I couldn't get your attention."

"Maybe we need to have another way for you to call me. Mom always gave us a bell to ring when we were sick. Remember?"

Abby nodded. "I'd like some lunch and a bell."

When Kate sat on the end of the bed, Abby pulled her feet away. The gesture made Kate wonder if she and her sister would ever be friends.

"I'd like a bowl of soup and crackers." Abby attempted to turn in bed, grudgingly accepting

Kate's aid when she discovered she couldn't complete the action by herself.

"What kind of soup?"

"Whatever you have."

"Chicken? Beef? Vegetables?"

"Whatever you have," Abby repeated.

Anything she chose wouldn't be right, but she'd try anyway.

While the chicken vegetable soup, which covered two of the categories, was heating, Kate searched the cabinet in the living room for a bell. Three little brass bells sat on the shelf, little Dutch girls with wide skirts her grandfather had brought home from World War Two. She picked one up, rang it and, once back in the kitchen, placed it on the tray she carried up to her sister's room.

After serving Abby, Kate looked through the freezer and pulled out a casserole to nuke for their dinner. Then she cut herself a piece of that wonderful red velvet cake and sat down, taking a deep breath, to relax.

As she savored the first bite of the delicious treat, she heard the bell, the sound growing louder and more demanding with each ring.

With a sigh, Kate put the fork down and stood. That jingling would get old very quickly.

Chapter Five

Once Abby was settled in bed and leaning against several pillows with the television remote in her hand, Kate called Rob.

"I'm ready to go to the hardware store. Is this a good time for you?"

"I'll be there in ten minutes."

And he was. Gone was the beat-up Chevy he'd had and loved to work on. In its place was a sleek dark green BMW.

As she opened the door and slid inside, Kate said, "This is much more comfortable than your motorcycle."

He laughed. "I haven't ridden the hog for years, not since I became a responsible husband, father and professional man with a practice too big to have time for such dangerous nonsense."

"Dangerous nonsense, huh?" She smiled at his teasing tone.

"Well, Lora has only one parent." His voice became serious, a shift that made her feel uncomfortable and insensitive. "I want to keep it that way."

She quickly wiped the smile from her lips. "Well, then, do you have time to work on your car?"

He shook his head, checked the street for traffic and pulled out. "Wish I did. Getting my hands greasy and fixing engines used to be one of my favorite things."

"Why don't you do that anymore?"

"Cars have changed." He stopped at the light and turned right as the traffic cleared. "Nowadays they all hook up to computers. The fun of working on a car was to tear it apart and figure out the problem without having a computer give me the answers."

"How 'bout old cars? Would you like to do restoration?"

What a difference the years made. Rob was the man with whom she'd shared her deepest hopes and wishes. Now they were talking about restoring cars.

But it was a start. As impatient as she was, she had to learn a new way of getting along with people, not continue with the surface contacts of her former life. The only way to restore relationships she'd left behind was little by little, one topic at a time, one conversation at a time, even if each had to do with restoring old cars.

He drove a few blocks in silence. "I've thought about that, but with Lora and work, I don't have the time. Besides, Mom lives in what used to be the garage. No space, either."

Obviously Rob's life had changed.

Once they arrived at the BuildersMart with the diagram of the pulley and handles from the physical therapist, Rob picked up the materials he needed and headed toward the checkout.

"Rob, just a minute." Kate stopped to consider her words. This was going to sound silly, but she had to ask. "Could you help me with something else?"

He turned. "What is it?"

"My dog, Coco…" The idea sounded so foolish, but the memory of the cocker attempting to climb onto the porch made her rush to finish. "She has arthritis and can't get up on the porch. I'd like to get her a ramp that would make that easy for her."

"You want a ramp for your dog?" His expression—head tilted and lips spread in a wide grin—was exactly what she'd expected.

With a slightly embarrassed nod, she said, "I know, but she's a sweet creature and we've been together a long time. Her hip really hurts her." She paused before saying the words she really didn't want to. "If she can't get up and down, I may have to…" She swallowed but couldn't complete the sentence.

"Hey, it's okay, Kate." His expression filled with concern. "Let's see what we can find."

What they found was a prefabricated ramp, little more than a narrow strip of metal and costing two hundred dollars. She tested the model on display. Not as sturdy as she'd hoped and far too expensive. "I don't know if she'd like this."

"You don't know if your dog would like this one?"

Kate glanced at him. He was smiling.

"No," she said. "It tilts a little. I don't think she'd feel secure. And her toenails would tap on the metal. She wouldn't like that."

Although he tried not to laugh, Kate could hear the amusement in his voice. "I'd hate for her to feel insecure." He drummed his fingers along the surface and listened to the ping of metal. "Or uncomfortable."

"I know it sounds silly…."

"It's okay." With a shake of his head, he added, "I've got bits and pieces of lumber. I'll build her a ramp that won't scare her."

"Oh, Rob, thank you. She'll be so grateful."

"Anything to gain Coco's gratitude." This time he didn't even try not to laugh.

After they'd paid Rob carried the bag to the car.

Silence fell between them on the ride back home. Searching for a topic of conversation, finally Kate asked, "Have you always had your office in Silver Lake?" Not an inspired question but at least it broke the quiet she'd found increasingly uncomfortable.

"No, after Junie and I married, we went to Atlanta where I interned with a firm. They offered me a position, but when we found out she was pregnant, we moved back to Silver Lake to raise our children." He paused for a few seconds before correcting himself. "To raise our daughter." He pulled into the driveway of the Victorian. "This is a great place for kids."

"I know. I remember." She closed her eyes for a moment to remember the joy of her childhood, then opened them to turn toward Rob. "Do you remember how much fun we had as kids, riding our bikes and playing hide-and-go-seek and chasing fireflies in the backyard during the summer?" She cupped her hands, remembering how she'd held the lightning bugs in the velvet softness of those warm evenings, how they lit up in her careful grasp, their wings beating gently against her fingers before she opened her hands to watch the trail of blinking light as they flew away.

"Yeah, you and Sara and I, always together." He popped the trunk, turned the ignition off and opened his door. "Have you seen Sara yet?"

Nodding, Kate opened the car door and stood. "For a few minutes at lunch. It was great although she wasn't happy I hadn't called her."

"And she let you know, I'm sure." Rob grabbed the package and followed Kate into the house. "I can put up the pulley for your sister now. When I have more time, I'll measure the porch to build the ramp."

"Let me check with Abby, see if it's all right for you to come upstairs now."

"It won't take more than five minutes to put the thing together," Rob called after her.

"It wouldn't be proper." Abby pulled the sheet over her shoulders and held it there with her left hand. "It wouldn't be at all proper for a man to come in here while I'm in bed."

"But, Abby." Kate stopped the words. Nothing she said would change her sister's mind. She knew that. She'd always known that. Why did she think today would be different? "Okay, let me help you stand. You can lie down in Brooke's room while Rob puts the pulley up."

Abby nodded and reached her left hand toward Kate. "But you keep the door open so I know there's nothing going on between you and Rob."

"Abby, there's nothing between Rob and me." Kate helped her sister turn in the bed and place her feet on the floor. As Abby stood and shoved her feet into her slippers, Kate steadied her. "We're old friends. I'm not staying long. He's changed. I've changed."

"I can stand by myself." Abby shrugged Kate's support away. "And I don't see you've changed all that much."

Kate watched Abby shuffle across the hall, her hand reaching for the wall for balance.

"I'll sit here at Brooke's desk." Abby settled herself in the cushioned chair and shut her eyes as she leaned back. "It feels good to sit up."

For a moment, Kate studied Abby. Although

her face was pale, the pallor belied her strength and sheer contrary stubbornness, a trait Kate feared they shared in equal amounts. Abby's dark hair had escaped from the usual braid and curled around her face making her look young and vulnerable, a side Kate didn't remember seeing in, well, many years. Not since Abby's boyfriend Joel had fallen for Kate. That had not been a good time.

Why should she feel guilty about Joel after all this time? As a self-centered sixteen-year-old, she'd flirted with Joel. Back then, all her friends were testing their newly found charms on young men, but "All my friends are doing it" was not a good excuse.

But she hadn't realized how much Abby cared about Joel until he'd broken up with Abby. When she'd heard Abby crying, Kate apologized. It hadn't helped. Nothing had. Her actions had reinforced her sister's certainty that Kate didn't care about anyone but herself. The whole mess had pretty well put the kibosh on any hope for sisterly closeness let alone a sliver of affection.

Another reason Kate had practiced flirtation with Joel was to capture Rob's attention. The plan had worked because Rob suddenly realized that his skinny friend from childhood had grown up. For six years there was no other man in her life but Rob. Actually Rob had been the only man she'd really cared about her entire life. Pitiful. Over the past twelve years, she should have fallen in love with someone else. Rob had.

"Kate?" His voice came from downstairs. "About ready?"

"Are you settled?" she asked Abby, who nodded but kept her eyes closed.

"We're ready. Come on up." Kate waited for him in the hall and pointed out the closet door in the master bedroom where the appliance was to be hung.

In seconds he'd attached the pulley to a rack he'd hung over the door, put the rope through the pulley and attached the handles. He pulled on each to make sure they fed easily.

"That should do it." He stood back to check the device and nodded. "It's a very simple machine but should do great in limbering up Abby's shoulder." As he headed out the bedroom door and down the hall, he said, "It's ready, Abby. Don't wear yourself out."

In response, Abby chuckled. A rusty, quiet sound but one of obvious amusement. "Thank you."

"I'll let myself out, Kate." His footsteps

clattered down the steps and across the hall. "When I get a chance, I'll be back to measure for the ramp."

Rob shrugged his shoulders, tense after an hour of sitting at the computer. After taking a long gulp of cold coffee, he stood and looked out the window. Outside, his daughter played on the swing with Timmy Hernandez from down the street. His mother watched and laughed with the children. He wished he were there now instead of working on this design.

He *had* to cut back on the workload. He *had* to learn to relax and schedule work so he could spend more time with Lora.

Yes, he needed to stop driving himself so hard, to slow down because the last few days he'd been on edge for some reason.

Too busy, that was the problem. After Junie died, he'd thrown himself into his work. Where was he two years later? Looking out the window at his daughter and wanting to push her on her swing and laugh with her. Lora was growing up. He wanted to share her childhood.

And, no matter how she attempted to hide it, his mother was aging. She walked more slowly and favored her right hip. When he asked her about it, she'd wave off his concern. She'd never admit to a weakness, especially not when she felt she had to take care of Lora. He'd been an only child, a late surprise to his forty-year-old parents. Now Mom was seventy-four. He shook his head. How could he have been so selfish that he expected her to raise his own child when she should have been able to just enjoy Lora, to spoil her like every other grandmother?

But left with an infant to raise after Junie's death, what choice did he have?

He picked up his handheld mobile device and opened his appointment calendar to see when he had time to kick back, to take Lora to the park and allow his mother time off. What was the worst thing that could happen if he cut back? Some other architect would get to design the new library.

Before he even glanced at the schedule, he flipped the PDA shut.

Who was he kidding? Yes, he was worried about his mother, but that wasn't the only thing bugging him. The demanding client who wanted a thirty-thousand-square-foot house that looked like a medieval castle on a half-acre plot of land wasn't what bothered him. Neither was it the delay on the house over in San Saba that made him short-tempered nor the expectation of the school board in Lampasas for him to complete the plans for the new middle school in three days.

The same thing was causing both his nerves and his mother's grumpiness.

Kate Wallace was back in town.

He turned toward the window, first glancing at the remodeled garage where his mother lived, its red brick outlined in white trim. Behind it and to his right was the Victorian house where he'd spent a lot of his time before he went to college. The house that had inspired him to become an architect so he could design buildings with the creative touches and the fine craftsmanship the old Victorian had. It was also the house where Kate had grown up, where they'd fallen in love. Right there on that broad back porch, listening to music from the Dkaneys' house, they'd watched the sky and the stars and discussed their future together for hours. Oh, and they had kissed once or twice during those deep discussions.

He'd gotten over that young love years ago. The first inkling that love didn't last forever, at least not Kate's, had hit him in college when Kate had visited a friend in Houston over spring break instead of coming home from UT to be with him. The final break had come after she graduated from college, when he had one more year of his five-year degree. She'd promised she'd come back after getting a master's in journalism from Columbia. They'd marry the next June.

Because by that time he knew she wouldn't return, the occasional phone calls, the many unanswered e-mails followed by weeks of silence hadn't hurt him as much as they had his loving and overly protective mother.

The mother who could never forgive Kate because she didn't understand that Kate had been the love of his youth but Junie had been the love of his life. He'd gotten over Kate's absence, but Junie's still tore him apart.

When Kate looked at him, he imagined she saw the same old Rob only years older. Same smile, same even temper.

The pencil he held broke with a loud crack.

The old Rob was the one who laughed easily, who lifted his infant daughter and hugged her, who'd loved his wife dearly and told her so in a hundred ways, who kidded his mother and told her not to worry. But the old Rob had been gone since he felt Junie's hand go limp in his. In that instant, he realized the woman he'd planned to spend forever with had left him.

The old Rob was the man everyone still saw when they looked at him.

No one ever caught sight of the Rob he was now.

He planned to keep it that way.

Kate watched from the hallway as Brooke glanced around the kitchen. Although she knew her mother was in bed upstairs, the girl still looked guilty when she put her plate on the floor for Coco to lick.

Within a few days, Coco had done what Kate couldn't. The dog had made a connection with Brooke, had made her laugh in a soft, self-conscious way but laugh nevertheless.

After Brooke picked up the plate, rinsed it and placed it inside the dishwasher, Kate entered the kitchen with her sister's tray.

"Looks like your mother is getting her appetite back." She placed the tray on the table and took the dishes to the sink.

Brooke nodded and wet the sponge to clean the counters.

"She did some exercises on the pulley Rob installed this morning. Hope that arm is going to heal up well."

With another nod, Brooke wiped off the top of the tray.

"Why don't you come outside with me and enjoy the breeze for a few minutes."

Halfway to the sink, Brooke stopped, absolutely still. "What?"

"I always loved sitting on the back porch. Mom and I used to spend time there, watch the sunset and just talk." Kate smiled at the memory. "Do you and your mother do that?"

The alien-visitor look was back in Brooke's eyes, as if Kate had no clue about her niece's life.

Sadly she did. She knew Brooke and Abby never sat on the back porch and talked about school and friends and fun. Did they ever talk?

The thought raised another concern: Did Brooke have any friends? Kate hadn't seen any over the few days she'd been here. "Would you like to invite some friends over to play sometime, Brooke?"

Her niece shook her head. "I don't have any…many friends."

The sentence broke Kate's heart. Every girl should have friends. Maybe she could talk to Sara about that. Or perhaps there was a group at church Brooke could join.

"Do you have to study tonight?" When Brooke didn't answer, Kate said, "Why don't you keep me company for a few minutes? Coco likes to sit on the porch, too."

At seven o'clock in early April, the light was beginning to fade. A soothing breeze ruffled Brooke's hair as she sat next to Kate in a porch chair. From the Dkanys' came the sound of Willie Nelson singing about being on the road again.

Kate watched as two boys rode their bikes on the strip of grass behind the house. Years ago, the alley between the houses had been used for trash collection with the truck stopping at the back gates of each house. Now, with each customer rolling trash bins down to the street every week, the alley had become a grassy passageway for neighbors between houses. Roses, trumpet vines and honeysuckle climbed the fences, which made it a lovely spot and, she thought as she took a deep breath, a fragrant one.

Coco spent almost fifteen minutes patrolling the fence, sticking her nose between slats to inspect the red and pink phlox growing on the other side before she waddled back to the porch and sat on the lawn, whimpering to be lifted.

"I'll get her." Brooke jumped to her feet and lifted Coco. She didn't place the dog on the porch but kept her in her arms to scratch her ears. Then she put Coco carefully on the porch and sat down. The pet put her head on Brooke's feet and fell asleep. Brooke fought a smile as she kept her eyes on the dog.

"Puppy." Kate heard a child's voice from the alley. Through the back gate and into the yard came a flash—a small flash in yellow shorts and a ruffled top. "I want to see Puppy."

"Hold on, Lora." Although Rob's legs were much longer than his daughter's, she had a head start. He caught up with her exactly as she pulled herself up on the porch and put her hand out toward the sleeping Coco. "Make sure the puppy is awake and knows you're here," he warned. "You don't want her to snap at you."

Not that the words seemed to make any difference to Lora. Struggling in her father's arms, she reached toward Coco. "Puppy."

Kate shook the dog gently. "Wake up, Coco. You have a visitor."

Rob put his daughter down. When the child patted Coco on the head, the dog smiled at her.

"I like Puppy," Lora said.

Brooke moved to sit next to Lora. "Coco loves to have her ears scratched right here." She showed the child a spot that caused the dog to snuffle in delight.

"It scares me how fast she can get away from me." Rob settled on the edge of the porch and kept his gaze on his daughter. His eyes filled with love. Then he reached out to place his hand on his daughter's shoulder. "She's fearless. I worry she'll get hurt."

For a moment Kate couldn't breathe. The bond between Rob and his daughter was so warm, so close. What had she given up for her few moments of fame?

Why on earth did she feel regret now?

He shook his head, then stood and pulled a measuring tape, a pad of paper and pencil from his pocket. "Show me where you want the ramp."

Kate got to her feet and indicated a place next to the steps. "Or maybe over there." She shook her head. "I'm not sure."

He smiled at her perplexed expression. "It's not that hard a decision. We're not building the Taj Mahal."

"I know. It's not even a filling station, but you know how touchy Abby… Never mind. Forget I said that. Do whatever you think is best."

"Yes, I know how touchy your sister can be." He nodded as he finished her thought. "Sometimes she has to be. She's had to keep up a registered landmark by herself, not easy with a house this old."

"Okay. You're right." She hated to admit any such thing. "Do you think we'll get in trouble with the historical commission for adding the ramp?"

"We can get away with a wood ramp off the back porch. I'll take it down as soon as you leave so it won't ruin the period charm."

He studied the area. "I think next to the steps is best." He nodded. "I don't think I'm going to have to go by the standard practice, which is one foot of ramp for every one inch of height." He pointed. "If I did that, the ramp would stretch pretty far out in the yard."

"Coco might never figure out what it's for."

"Oh?" He smiled again, an expression which made Kate's heart flutter.

How stupid was that reaction?

"Not a bright dog?"

"She's a cocker spaniel, a breed known for being cute not smart."

"Then I'll make it short but still at an easy climb so she can get up." He took some measurements and wrote them on the notepad, then pointed. "Might want to put an edge on the side so she doesn't fall off."

"Probably a good idea."

"Cute, not smart." He flipped the pad shut. "I'll cut some wood and be back in an hour or so."

She glanced at the sky. "It'll be pretty dark by then."

"This is not hard to do." He smiled at his daughter, who scratched Coco. "I'll take her home and put her, to bed, then be back with the lumber and get started."

The love in his eyes when he watched his daughter again awakened the foolish regret. Why? She'd left Rob and Silver Lake behind with no remorse years ago and she'd be leaving again as soon as her sister had healed enough to get around and she got a job. But no matter what she told herself, the foolish pang of regret refused to go away.

That's why she turned the porch lights on an hour later so Rob could work but didn't go outside.

Instead she watched his progress from the window over the sink. She couldn't take her eyes from him, from his broad shoulders, from the muscles that tightened under his T-shirt when he swung the hammer, from the man he'd become. And she stayed there, watching, for ten minutes as he pounded nails and attached the lumber to the frame.

"Aunt Kate?" Brooke's voice came from behind her. "What are you doing?" Her niece looked over Kate's shoulder then her eyes shifted quickly to Kate's face. "Watching Rob build the ramp?"

"Yes, I'm pleased it's going so fast. Coco will be happy."

But Brooke's eyes didn't leave Kate's face and she didn't think the child was buying her story. Why should she? Here Kate stood, not washing a dish or filling a glass with water, just standing by the window, enjoying the sight of a gorgeous man working in the backyard.

Surely Brooke wouldn't realize what Kate was doing.

Her hopes were dashed when Brooke said, "Why are you watching him?"

What could she say? "I really appreciate that he's building the ramp for Coco." There, that sounded good. Better than, "I like to watch the muscles in his shoulders while he hammers."

"Why don't you sit outside instead of watching from in here?"

"Cooler in here."

"Weren't you going to marry Rob before you left?"

"That was a long time ago."

Before Brooke could ask another question, Rob stood and shouted, "Kate, I'm going home. Your dog can use the ramp the way it is. I'll put the edge on and finish it later."

"Thank you," she called back to him before she turned to face her niece and smiled like a loving aunt.

Brooke looked at her, head titled. The child didn't buy her aunt's lack of interest. Not at all.

And neither did Kate. Try as she might, neither did Kate.

Chapter Six

For at least the fifth or sixth time that Thursday morning Kate descended the stairs from her sister's bedroom. Below her waited Coco, asleep on the rug Kate had placed next to the newel post. There the cocker kept vigil when Kate disappeared up the steps.

Under what Kate jokingly called "her supervision," Abby exercised her shoulders six times a day, every two and a half hours for twenty minutes each. During the total of two hours the sisters had spent together every day for the past two days, not a word of conversation passed between them. Kate had attempted to break the silence with questions like, "How does that feel?" or "Can you feel any difference in the level of motion?"

But Abby didn't respond.

Oh, occasionally she would say something like, "Hand me the cane" or "The rope's hung up in the pulley" or "The correct term is range of motion." Other than that, silence lay between them, thick as the elastic bands Abby used to exercise and twice as taut.

This time, Kate escaped from the physical therapy program at one o'clock in the afternoon. When she hurried into the kitchen with Coco on her heels, Sara awaited, ensconced at the kitchen table, sipping from one glass of iced tea while she pushed the other toward Kate.

"You look as if you could use something to drink."

"Thank you." Kate picked up the glass to enjoy a deep gulp, then set it down. "And thanks for coming by for lunch." She pulled out the salads she'd prepared earlier and placed them on the table. After she finished putting together the meal, she sat down across from her friend.

"Grace?" Sara took Kate's hand. "I want to say a prayer over our meal." Bowing her head, she said, "Most Loving God, for friends and food, for sharing and caring, for your eternal generosity, we thank you. Amen."

Kate didn't know how to begin a conversation about her niece, so instead she asked, "Why don't you tell me about your kids?"

"Oh, yes, my kids." Sara grinned and reached for her billfold to open it to a picture and pass it across the table. "Those are my daughters, Marisol and Rosita. They're fifteen and twelve and I love them dearly. We're a family."

Tall and slender, Marisol had dark shoulder-length hair. Rosita had beautiful mocha skin and dark eyes. "Where did they come from?" Kate shook her head in confusion. "They're adopted?"

"Of course they're adopted. You've only been gone twelve years." Sara laughed. "I've been a foster mother for five years and have taken in fifteen, maybe twenty kids. It took three years before Marisol's and Rosita's parents surrendered rights. By that time, they were too old for most people to adopt so I was blessed to get them."

"They are beautiful and very fortunate." Kate passed the picture back. "They really are, and I want to meet them."

"I have my girls and also two foster girls. Keeps me busy."

"How do you find time to do all that?"

"Priorities. I make time. I heard about the

need for foster families in church one Sunday and decided this is what I'm called to do. A few weeks later, I hired another recent A&M graduate and cut back on my time in the office so I'm home in the evening and most weekends, unless there's an inconsiderate cow having a difficult birth."

Sara put the pictures back. "Okay." She leaned forward. "My thought is that you didn't ask me here to talk about my kids, although I could go on forever. So tell me, why did you invite me to lunch?"

"Maybe I shouldn't even talk to you about this." She glanced at Sara. "I mean, I'm not going to be here long. It's probably none of my business, but I'm really worried."

"Do you have a question in there some-place?" Sara tilted her head. "Do you want to talk to me about Rob?"

"About Rob?" Kate shook her head. "No, of course not. Why would I do that?"

"Maybe because you were crazy about him in high school and you're back and you're both single now?"

"Sara, I'm not back, not really. I'm leaving when Abby's better and have no desire to start a relationship of any kind with a man, any man, not for the short time I'll be here."

"Well, if you did, I thought I should warn you."

Kate frowned. "Warn me about what?"

"Rob. He's still mourning his wife."

"After two years? He looks fine to me."

"*Claro que sí.* Of course he looks fine. He looked fine after you ran out on him, too, but I know the signs."

"I'm not interested in him." For a second, the sight of Rob's dark, handsome face and wide shoulders flickered through her imagination. "Not a bit," she said precisely in a quick effort to rid her brain of that vision.

Sara watched her closely but didn't say anything more although Kate could tell she wanted to.

With a sigh, Kate said, "It's Brooke, my niece."

"What about her?"

Kate struggled to find the words. How to discuss Brooke without discussing Abby? "She seems so sad and has no friends. I don't know what to do or even if I should interfere." Kate bit her lip. "I'm worried about her. I hope you can help, at least give me some advice. As the mother of teenagers, you must be filled with wisdom."

"Hardly that. Mothers of teenagers know very little, at least that's what the kids say."

Sara smiled. "Of course you have a right to help her. Brooke's your niece, Kate, she's family. You don't want her to grow up unhappy."

"Okay." She took a long drink of coffee. "But what do I do? How can I help her be more normal, make some friends?"

"How old is she?"

"Nine."

Sara thought for a moment. "One of my foster kids, Marta Elisa, is eight. She's a sweetheart." Sara pulled out a calendar and studied it for a few seconds. "Can you bring Brooke over Saturday afternoon for an hour or two? I know you can't leave Abby alone for long, but my neighbor has a pool she lets us use. We could all go swimming. Maybe that would help."

"Oh, Sara, thank you."

"No, I should have thought of it myself." She glanced at the calendar again. "Also, we have a junior fellowship group at church for third through sixth grade. It meets Sunday evenings. Bring her. I'm one of the sponsors and the two younger girls go."

"That all sounds wonderful. I knew you'd figure out something." Kate breathed a sigh of relief. "I don't know how to thank you."

Sara finished the last bite of her salad,

savoring the taste for a few seconds. "How's Abby doing?"

Kate shrugged. "Okay. I guess."

"I imagine she hates to show how much she needs you."

"Well, that's part of it, I'm sure, but we're sisters and yet…" She paused. "We should need each other. We should be able to accept each other."

"Being related doesn't guarantee closeness or friendship."

"Yes, but…" Kate shook her head. "I know sometimes blood ties don't mean anything, but I'd like to be part of a family again, at least have a sister I can chat with."

"Well." Sara reached across the table to place her hand on Kate's. "You've got me."

"Thank you. I'm very fortunate for that."

"You won't forget it again, right?"

"I'll never forget that. That's a promise."

After dinner, with Abby settled, Kate clipped the leash on Coco and invited Brooke to walk with them. "It's not hard," she told her niece. "She walks very slowly."

"Then why do you do it?" Brooke scowled as she started the dishwasher.

"Just try it. You may enjoy it."

They strolled through the falling twilight with the crickets playing a courting song and a gentle breeze ruffling her hair. Brooke, a few feet in front of Kate, held Coco's leash. With a wave, Kate greeted her neighbors, who rocked on their front porches and enjoyed the cool air.

"Dear Lord, thank you," she whispered, overwhelmed by the familiar beauty of her hometown.

If she loved the place so much, why did she plan to leave as soon as she could?

After a trip around the block, they entered the house. Brooke pulled up a chair at the kitchen table to do homework, Coco settled at her feet, and Kate poured a glass of tea. "I'm going to take this up to your mother and see if she needs anything else."

"Wouldn't it be easier if her bed was down here?"

Kate wanted to say, "Of course, but she's stubborn," but bit back the words and said, "She's more comfortable there."

"Oh, sure." Brooke rolled her eyes, then went back to her math.

It was after eight that evening by the time Coco followed Kate out to the backyard. While the dog carefully descended the steps and sniffed around the fence, Kate settled in the chair and sipped her tea. After only a few minutes, she heard a rustling in the grassy alley and the gate swung open.

"Who is it?" Kate called as she flipped on the yard light.

"Puppy!" came the answer, which made more sense when the voice of a young child added, "Want to see Puppy."

"What are you doing out so late, Lora?" Kate stood and stepped off the porch toward the child while Coco wagged her tail in delight when she saw her friend. "Where are your father and grandmother?"

"Puppy." Lora reached out to scratch Coco's ears.

As she got closer to Rob's daughter, she saw the child wore a pink cotton nightgown and matching furry slippers.

"Lora, why are you here? Are you supposed to be in bed?"

The child shook her head just as Kate heard voices from the Chambers's backyard.

"Lora?"

"Rob, she's down here." Kate watched the child as she heard someone running down the pathway between the houses. "She's in my backyard."

For a moment, Lora looked up, eyes wide and worried, before she dropped her attention to the dog.

"Lora," Rob said as he pushed through the gate. "What are you doing here?"

"Puppy." She smiled at him, an expression of innocent sweetness sure to melt the hardest of hearts.

Except, at this moment, her father's.

Rob rubbed his forehead. "I don't know what to do with her, Kate." He studied his daughter. "After she finished her bath and put on her gown, I got a phone call. When I went in her bedroom to tuck her in only a couple of minutes later, she wasn't there. She wasn't anywhere in the house or at Mom's apartment."

He sat on the edge of the porch and shook his head. "I don't know how to get through to her. She doesn't recognize the concept of danger and is so hardheaded. I've talked to her and scolded and explained, but it doesn't do any good."

What made Kate think she'd do any better? Well, from what Rob said, she couldn't do worse.

"Lora." She kneeled to be on eye level with the child. "This is my house and my yard."

"No." Lora shook her head. "You don't live here."

"And she's too smart for her own good," Rob muttered.

"Yes, this is my house and my dog."

Lora considered this for a moment. "Your puppy."

"Yes, and you don't have my permission to visit my puppy by yourself."

"Pweese?"

Because this was the first time she'd heard Lora speak like a baby, Kate was pretty sure the child had used both the word and the pitiful, pleading look successfully before.

"Lora, this is not your house. You cannot come in the yard by yourself and without permission."

"Okay," she chirped with what even Kate could tell was a complete lack of sincerity.

"Well, that was a waste of time." She stood.

"If her stubbornness didn't worry me so much, I'd laugh at your efforts." Rob's expression as he watched his daughter was filled with love and exasperation. "I don't know what to do with her."

Kate reached down and picked up Coco. "Lora," she said sternly. "This is *my* dog. You cannot visit or pet my dog without *my* permission."

"Pweese?"

"No. You can only play with *my* dog if your father or grandmother asks me first."

Lora frowned, then turned another winning smile toward Kate. "Pweese?" When Kate's face showed no warming, Lora sighed. "Okay."

"You are to come here to see the puppy only if your grandmother or father call and ask me." Kate paused. "Do you understand that?"

Lora nodded. "Pet Puppy now?"

"No, Lora." Rob took the child's hand. "It's time for bed." He led her toward the gate.

"Bye, Puppy." Lora waved. "Bye, Puppy's mommy."

Puppy's mommy? That's who she was? She'd dropped from serving as press secretary for a powerful congressman to Coco's mother? How the mighty have fallen. Or, perhaps, this was a step up? Whichever it was, she smiled.

"Good night, Puppy's mommy," Brooke called from the porch. Then her niece did something startling. She laughed.

Wonder of all wonders. Brooke had made a joke and laughed.

With a grin for her niece, Kate strolled toward the gate to watch Rob carry Lora toward their house.

A few fireflies were beginning to glow and the honeysuckle smelled sweet. Hanging from the Norton house behind her were pots of geraniums, which reminded her again of the beauty her mother had created, how much it had meant to her.

So what if she wouldn't be here long? She was here now, and she could start a garden. Maybe she'd ask Brooke to help her with it.

If no one wanted to keep it up after she left, that was okay. She could start it, which was more than she'd done with the book she'd considered writing about her experiences over the past year. *Considered* was all she'd done about it. The idea no longer seemed as interesting as it had during the trial when she'd wanted to tell her side of the mess.

Here the beauty of Silver Lake enveloped her. The thought of planting and caring for a garden filled her with a long-absent and very much missed sense of purpose.

She'd do it.

Chapter Seven

Lora skipped through the backyard of the Wallace house, her laughter ringing as she followed Coco across the thick grass. Because one of her hops equaled several of the dog's creaky steps, she danced in circles around the cocker. Rob grinned as he watched her, filled with the warmth his daughter always brought to a heart that hadn't wanted to feel for a long time.

"I thought I'd make the edge about two inches high." He showed Kate the length between his thumb and index finger, then glanced at where she sat on the edge of the porch. "What do you think?"

As he kneeled on the ground next to her, Rob couldn't help but notice what a very nice distraction Kate made in her white shorts, blue

T-shirt and sparkly sandals that showed pink toenails.

He liked her hair this way, short and casual. When she'd been Miss Mesa County, she'd worn it long and curly. Nice, but it looked good sort of waving back. Back then, she'd had light blond hair, but it had darkened. He liked that, too.

In fact, if he wanted a woman in his life, she looked perfect for the part. But he wasn't hanging out for a woman. If he were, Kate Wallace would be the last one he'd choose. She couldn't be relied on.

After a few minutes of consideration while he laughed at his daughter's antics, he realized as attractive as he found Kate, he wasn't ready for anything that took him outside the parameters he'd imposed on himself. Actually the boundaries that life had forced on him to keep him safe, to keep from going through what he had when Junie died. He wouldn't risk that again. Ever.

Nonetheless, enjoying how Kate looked, taking in her short hair and long legs was pleasant. Extremely pleasant. He could still enjoy the sight of a pretty woman. None of that made any promises, certainly didn't demand he consider a future with that woman or any woman.

Kate stood and took a step off the porch to stand next to him and survey the area. "Looks good."

"Miss Kate." Lora finished running a circuit of the yard and stopped in front of her. "Puppy's asleep." She waved toward Coco. Worn-out, the dog had curled up beneath the tree.

"I'm glad you came to visit her." Kate leaned down and smiled into the child's face, a tender expression like none Rob had seen in her eyes. "Your father called and asked if you could come see the dog with him. I'm glad you followed the rules." She straightened. "Rob, would it be all right if Lora had a cookie?"

"Oh, yes, yes, yes." Lora hopped, her red ringlets bouncing, while she sang, "Cookie, cookie, cookie."

What a blessing she was.

"It's too late to turn that down now." Rob laughed. "Mom and I spell a lot because once a word is spoken, we can't change our minds."

"Daddy, come with me." While Kate disappeared inside, Lora took Rob's hand and led him up on the porch and to the chairs. "Wait for Miss Kate." She pushed him to sit down first, then reached out for him to lift her onto his lap.

Once there she pulled herself over to kneel in his lap and put her head on his shoulder. Rob recognized the position immediately. Lora wanted something and was softening him up with her hug.

"Daddy, Lora wants a puppy."

"Yes, kitten, I know you do." He felt her relax in his arms. "But we've talked about this before, and your grandmother and I…" He realized that her squirmy little body had gone still and sagged against his chest. That was Lora: running like a very short, toddling sprinter one minute, taking a nap the next.

Kate shoved the screen open with her shoulder and carried a tray to the table between the chairs. "Sorry I took so long, but I got a glass of lemonade for all of us and a plate of cookies. I hope…" She paused when she spotted the sleeping child. "I didn't wake her up, did I?"

"No, she's out for a few minutes, but she'll wake up full of energy and chattering in no time." He shifted Lora so her legs lay across his lap, her head still against his shoulder. "Don't suppose you'd mind handing me a glass?"

For a few minutes, they sat in silence.

"I'm thinking of putting in a few flowers."

She waved her hand toward the fenced area. "But I don't know what will work." She took a sip from her glass. "Do you remember how beautiful mother's garden was?"

He nodded. "Everyone in town missed her when she died, but when her flowers didn't bloom the next spring, we felt the loss all over again."

She cleared her throat. "I don't know what to start with. Maybe some geraniums and impatiens with ground cover over in the corner."

"In June, the heat will kill the impatiens." He put his glass on the table and shifted a little, making sure Lora was comfortable. "Of course, you don't have to worry because you won't be around in June."

"No, I probably won't."

"Then why would you want to plant a garden?"

"I don't know." She shrugged. "Just a thought. Maybe to remember Mom. Maybe to get out of the house."

After a minute of silence and listening to Lora's deep breathing, Rob laughed.

"What is it?" Kate glanced at him.

"Something I wondered." He smiled at Kate. "Would you mind if I asked you a personal question?"

When she glanced at him, apprehension obvious in her wide eyes, he added, "No, not *really* personal. I only wondered why you have that ugly old car." He shook his head. "You were going to burn up the world, become rich and famous. For a while you did pretty well. I'd say you are probably the most famous and successful citizen of Silver Lake, and I'd have expected you to have a new car, shiny and expensive."

She nodded. "I did, too. Life didn't turn out exactly as I'd planned." She focused her gaze on the yard. "I bought that car a year after I got to Houston. I'd begun to make money but couldn't afford a new car, the type I thought someone with my future should have." She shook her head. "See, I never changed. I've always been pretentious and overconfident." She grinned at her words. "This one was five years old when I bought her, but in great shape, although you may not believe that seeing her now."

"Hey, it's eleven years later. I believe it."

"The heat and humidity of Houston and Miami aren't kind to car paint and fabric tops." She took a long sip of the lemonade. "I'd planned to buy a new one when I got the offer to work for Congressman Smythe in Florida three years ago. It was exactly the job I wanted, but the move and the new clothes and the condo all cost a lot. The car? Well, I could get along with the old car." After a long pause, she continued. "When I had enough money and was fixin' to replace the Lexus, I found out about the kickbacks and bribes my boss had taken. I quit."

"Good choice."

"I think so." She shrugged. "I couldn't work for him anymore, but when I quit, he black-listed me, ruined my reputation. No one else would hire me and the prosecutors wouldn't let me leave Florida. It's been a long and lean year. All I have left is Coco, a storage unit full of stuff in Miami, a little money in savings and a car that usually runs."

"So no new car."

"No new car, no new clothes, no condo, no job."

"Friends?"

"Amazing how that is. As soon as I became an outcast, my friends acted as if they'd never known me. A few told me they respected me for what I did but not to count on them to stand up for me. It was as if they'd never known me." Her gaze flickered away from him. "The man I'd been dating for a year was a member of the congress-man's team."

Rob pushed down the wave of interest followed by a touch of—it couldn't be—jealousy that hit him like a punch in the stomach when she talked about a past boy-friend.

"He told me I was nuts and was furious because I'd cost him his job. I guess the worst part is that he couldn't understand why I did what I did." She sighed. "He asked why couldn't I just shut up and accept that con-gressmen taking bribes—happens all the time. And when I decided to testify—not that I had much choice—he was really angry."

"It must have been hard."

She nodded. "What hurts so much is that after all the hard work, I have to start over." She blinked tears away. "I gave up so much and ended up with so little." Her eyes fell on Lora. "Nothing that really lasted. Nothing that matters now."

He had no idea how to respond to that, but as the silence stretched out between them, he said, "Your parents would have been proud. You stood up for what you thought was right."

She nodded, her eyes shifting back to look at the shed.

"It couldn't have been easy."

"It wasn't." She took a bite of cookie, chewed and swallowed. Then she straightened and her voice became brisk. "All of that explains why I have my old car and why I'm back home without a lot of money."

He felt Lora stir. Her hand reached out and patted his cheek, then she pushed away from him and wiggled off his lap. "Come on, Daddy. Let's go home. Play with Grandma." She jumped off his lap and pulled his hand. "Say 'Bye-bye,' to Puppy." Before she took off, Lora ran to the table and grabbed a cookie. "Thank you, Puppy's mommy."

Rob stood. "She's always busy, always going from one place to another."

Lora jumped from the porch, skipped to Coco, her feet making soft thuds on the grass. "Bye, Puppy." When she rubbed her hand over the dog's head, Coco noticed the cookie only inches from her nose. With a practiced move, the cocker pulled it from Lora's fingers and gulped it down.

"Daddy," the child shouted. "Daddy, Puppy took my cookie." Tears gathered in her eyes.

"Take her two." Kate wrapped a couple of cookies in a napkin. "But hold them up high," she told Lora. "Coco loves cookies almost as much as she loves little girls."

When her gaze again fell on Lora, Rob wondered if children were one of the things Kate regretted giving up.

"Aunt Kate." Brooke's voice came through the screen door from the kitchen. "When are we going swimming?"

"Swimming?" Rob repeated as Lora pulled him across the yard. "Sounds fun. Where?"

"Sara invited us. She says her neighbors have a pool."

"Have a great time." He waved as he turned down the grassy alleyway between the homes. "Bye, Puppy's mommy. Bye, Puppy's sister."

Kate held in a laugh that threatened to explode when Brooke repeated, "Puppy's sister?"

"It's a great honor," Kate said. "Okay, we're supposed to be there about noon today." She glanced at her watch and jumped up from her chair. "Didn't realize it was eleven-thirty. I'll clean up this stuff—" she picked up the cookies and glasses "—and check on your mother. Then let's put on our suits." She dashed into the house. "I grabbed some chips and a cake at the H-E-B yesterday so we have plenty of food."

With a bowl of soup and a plate of sand-wiches on a tray, Kate knocked on the door to her sister's room. "I have lunch, Abby." Hearing nothing, she opened the door a crack and peeked inside to see Abby reading. "I have your lunch," she repeated. "May I come in?"

Abby nodded.

"Wouldn't you prefer to have your lunch here at the table instead of in bed?" Kate put the tray down and pulled a chair out.

Abby sat up, turned in bed and stood.

"You know," Kate said as Abby sat, "we'd love to have you join us for dinner."

"Maybe. Once the doctor says it's all right. I won't intrude until then."

"I'm sure…" Kate stopped in midsentence. She wasn't sure and had no reason to argue. Besides, getting her sister out of bed and eating at the table constituted an important beginning. "If you have everything, Brooke and I are leaving now."

Abby nodded again.

As Kate hurried to get ready, thoughts of Abby's constant bad temper bothered her. When her sister was a child, she'd figured Abby was just a grouch, but her grumpy mood had lasted a lifetime, at least the lifetime Kate had known her. Had she ever been happy? Had her wedding been happy? Had she rejoiced at the birth of her daughter?

And if so, how had that joy disappeared so completely? Was it from the shoulder pain?

No, if that were the answer, Brooke wouldn't be such a sad child and other people in town would have rushed to help Abby.

Then Brooke's voice pierced her thoughts. "Let's go, Aunt Kate," Brooke shouted happily from the front yard. "I put Coco in the backyard and gave her water." When Kate ran out the front door, Brooke added, "We're going to walk. It's only a few blocks." Her glance at the car repeated her earlier statement. She wouldn't be caught dead in that thing.

But Brooke was happy. For that, Kate would walk a hundred blocks.

On the morning of Palm Sunday, the pageant of Jesus riding into the city on a donkey was reenacted by the youth group while the congregation waved palms. After that, everyone except the donkey entered the sanctuary still rejoicing.

As Kate waited for the procession to begin, Rob appeared next to her. "Do you remember when we were the kids who used to do this?" he asked. "Do you remember when I tried to ride in victory?"

"How could I forget? How could any of us? How old were you?"

"Twelve, thirteen?"

"As I recall, the donkey didn't want to get close to all those waving palms and took off down Goliad Street with you hanging on."

"For my life." Rob shook his head. "That donkey moved faster than any horse I've ever ridden."

When church started, Brooke pulled her aunt down the aisle toward her new friends. The swimming party had been fun. Sara's kids had welcomed Brooke and introduced her to their friends. When one of the children shoved Brooke in the pool, her scream was filled with the delight of acceptance. Kate sat next to Sara and looked around the congregation, amazed at how much at home she felt here. The town had begun to pull her in, exactly the opposite of how she'd felt when she was younger and tugging in the other direction.

After the service, Mrs. Watkins, beautiful in a pale blue suit and matching wide-brimmed hat, gestured with her beautiful French-tipped nails and said, "I've still got that job open. We need a good reporter."

Kate had hoped Mrs. Watkins had given up. A job in a small-town newspaper wasn't what Kate wanted in her life now. Probably not ever.

Well, most probably never.

* * *

That same Sunday evening, Rob pulled the sheet over Lora and bent to kiss her pink cheek. "Say your prayers, Kitten."

"Dear God up in heaven, thank you for the beautiful day. Bless Grandma and Daddy and Puppy and help me be a good girl. Amen."

Rob grinned when his daughter added Coco to her prayer. Someday he would think about getting her a puppy. Maybe when Coco left.

By the time he'd reached the hallway, Lora was asleep. He headed toward his office, planning to finish a set of plans he'd present later in the week. As he pulled the shades down, he saw the porch where Kate sat looking comfortable and very peaceful, Coco sleeping at her feet.

A longing to join her hit him with an unexpected jolt. He recognized only too well the danger of thinking about Kate. At this moment, he didn't care. She'd be gone in a few weeks. There was no chance they'd become involved over such a short time. She wasn't interested and he, well, neither was he.

Besides, she looked different and was different. After all she'd been through with her jobs and her life and her useless friends, she'd probably changed as much inside as she had outside. This Kate wasn't the Kate he'd been in love with. She was more mature, more experienced and more focused. After the time spent in big cities, Silver Lake wouldn't appeal to her anymore. Neither would a small-town architect when she'd been in circles of power.

But he was lonely, so alone at this moment he didn't really care what happened in a few minutes or a few weeks.

He turned the light out and headed out the back door. Like a good carpenter, he needed to check out his project, see how the ramp worked. To see if it needed a coat of water-resistant paint.

Who was he kidding? The ramp was fine. As for Kate, when she left again, this time he knew that would happen and wouldn't allow himself to care. This time he'd guard his heart.

What was wrong with a light flirtation with a pretty neighbor?

Tired of lame excuses and complicated rationalizations, he shut off his brain and strolled across his backyard.

Chapter Eight

"Nice night."

Kate started when Rob's hand fell on her shoulder. He jerked it away immediately, but not before an unwanted warmth lingered there. "Hey." She looked back at him. "I didn't hear you coming."

"Wrapped up in your thoughts?"

"Probably, although I may have been asleep." She laughed. "Sit down." She waved toward the chair next to her. "It's so quiet here, I get a lot of thinking done. More than I have for years."

As he sat, Rob moved the chair an inch, only a little bit, away from her. "How does the ramp work?"

Well, that was a sudden change in direction. If she'd thought he'd delve into her thoughts or ask what she'd been considering, she was seriously mistaken and many years too late to expect that.

"Great." She reached down to wake the cocker. "Coco, come show Rob how you use your ramp."

Coco opened her eyes, woofed, then fell back to sleep again. Even with a light nudge, the dog refused to move.

"You probably won't believe it now, but it was a big hit. You should have seen her when she figured out what it was for. Up and down, up and down. She was as excited as she ever gets these days."

She picked Coco up, carried her to the bottom of the ramp and put her on the ground. "Show Rob how much you like it." Coco dropped onto her behind and smiled up at Kate but made no move to climb the ramp. "Sorry." Kate laughed. "We'll try this another day." She walked back to the porch while Coco took off to explore.

He watched the cocker's progress around the yard before he turned to ask, "What were you thinking about?"

Nice of him to ask, although he sounded as if he didn't care that much. Probably being polite. However, Rob wasn't the person to discuss her future with. They'd done that before, and she'd carried through with none of those plans, only the ones she'd hidden inside her.

And, although he had a daughter, she didn't think he'd understand and be of any help with the problems facing Brooke, a much older child.

"It's Abby." She finally settled on that worry. "You and she—well, the two of you get along much better than she and I ever have, better than anyone I've ever seen Abby with. Why? Why does she accept your teasing and your advice?"

"Simple. You know Charley Granger and I played football and basketball together in high school."

"I remember. Charley's a great guy."

"When he was courting Abby and Junie and I were dating, we went out together a lot. The four of us were good friends, but their marriage didn't last long. I know what she went through. I was there for both Charley and your sister. Not an easy time for either." He shrugged. "I guess she appreciates that and lets me get away with what no one else can."

"What happened between them?"

He stood, put his hands in his pockets and looked down. "Can't tell you that. Confidential."

What he could have said without being out of line was that if she wanted to know what happened in her sister's life, she should've been here.

The firm line of his jaw and the width of his shoulders stood out against the pale sky. Rob looked determined and loyal and incredibly masculine and handsome. For an odd reason, Kate was more drawn to the first two characteristics than his strong good looks. What an idiot—alone with a gorgeous guy just as evening fell and she found loyalty more important than looks? She must be getting old.

He gazed at her, the light stubble on his chin showing dark and the expression in his eyes veiled. When had Rob begun to look dark and dangerous? Hadn't he always been the nice guy, the open guy?

Not now. His stance showed he'd shut her out completely. He'd posted No Trespassing signs that couldn't be more clear.

"I understand. Thanks for giving me a little insight. Would you like…" But before she could finish the statement, the jingling of the bell interrupted her words. "I have to see what Abby wants. Thanks again, for the ramp and the information."

She watched him head off in the dusk for a

few seconds before the bell sounded again. With a sigh, she turned back to the house and pulled the screen door open.

Friday night, almost two weeks after Kate's arrival, Brooke spent the night at Sara's. Kate wished she could have had Marta Elisa spend the night here, but Abby—well, Abby wouldn't take kindly to the giggles of two little girls at midnight.

Sunday morning, Brooke pulled Kate out of bed at six to go to the community Easter sunrise service in the church parking lot. The sun had risen long before seven o'clock, but the light shimmered in the cedars and pierced the leaves of the post oak to lay a lacy mat over the worshippers.

In the field behind the church, brilliant coreopsis, what her mother had called golden wave, stood a foot high, their yellow petals and red-brown centers glowing in the morning sun. Bluebonnets, magenta wine cups, yellow-red Indian blankets with their dark red centers and a few tall red Indian paintbrushes covered the field like a Persian rug.

Kate's heart swelled when the miracle of Easter was retold and the familiar Bible verses were read. As the congregation joined together to proclaim, "Hallelujah, He is risen," the words echoed in her soul.

How could she have allowed her faith to lapse when this moment of shining victory filled her with such amazement, such joy, such depth of feeling? "Hallelujah," she whispered and felt the words reach into the depths of her soul. "He has risen," she proclaimed with the rest of the worshippers.

Even the knowledge she had to go home and help Abby couldn't dim the radiance that filled Kate. In fact, the depth of faith that echoed within her pointed out her shortcomings and filled her with the strength to change. "Oh, risen Lord, please help me do better, to be better," she whispered as the congregation sang "Christ the Lord Has Risen Today."

She knew she couldn't wait. She realized it was up to her to make peace with her sister. She didn't know how, but she had to because her faith demanded it.

The next morning, Kate drove Abby home from her appointment with the doctor.

Two weeks. She'd been in Silver Lake for over two weeks and felt as if she'd never left, had trouble remembering the life she'd led before.

As she gave the engine a little more gas, it skipped a beat and gasped. Would her old Lexus finally quit on her?

"We should have taken my car." Abby cradled her arm and glared at her sister.

"We probably should have, but we'll be fine." The engine sputtered before running smoothly again. "Brooke tells me the church is having a picnic and service out at the lake in a few weeks. Maybe you'll feel up to going."

"If I feel well enough to do anything, I'd be going to work."

"I'd like to take Brooke."

"Go ahead. I'll get along fine without you."

"Yes, I know." And Kate did, but she wished she could hear some warmth in her sister's words, gratitude for taking care of her when she couldn't get out of bed by herself or cook for herself or do much of anything else.

Not that she'd expected even the smallest gesture of appreciation. After all, she hadn't come back to Silver Lake because she was a loving sister, and Abby knew that good and well. Kate should be grateful her sister didn't throw that in her face at every opportunity.

"You got a good report from the doctor. He

says you're recovering a lot of your range of motion." Kate checked the traffic and turned onto the highway.

"He also said six more weeks out of work. Six more weeks with this immobilizer and not being able to take care of myself."

Although she didn't say it, Kate could guess the rest of Abby's thoughts. "Six more weeks of having my little sister take care of me."

"I'm thinking about hanging geraniums on the porches around the house."

"Thought you were going to plant a garden."

"It didn't work out. I tried, but I don't have mother's gift."

"Or her stick-to-it attitude. Make you dig a little dirt, sweat a little and you turn tail."

Kate bit her lip. She didn't want to pick a fight with her sister, not out here on the highway. In fact, not anyplace if she was trying to make peace between them.

Besides, they had to get along for six weeks—only forty-two more days!—then she'd be out of Silver Lake and back to her life. Her real life. Not that she knew what it was yet.

Why did the thought fill her with panic and with sadness?

Kate reminded herself that six weeks was also the amount of time she had to reconcile with her sister. Only forty-two days when they hadn't learned to get along in thirty-four years.

As for what Abby said about Kate's never completing anything, her words contained a lot of truth. Only a few days earlier, Kate had gotten a shovel out, attempted to turn over the dirt in the corner of the yard and broke a nail while perspiration dripped into her eyes. When her shoulders and legs had ached so much she couldn't sleep last night, Kate realized that grand plan wouldn't work, either. Hanging pots of geraniums would be lovely and a lot less trouble.

The next four evenings, Kate sat out on the porch. Once she'd brought a book, but insects gathered when she turned on the porch light so she didn't try that again. Every evening, she sang along to whatever music the Dkaneys listened to.

One evening Mrs. Chambers brought Lora over. While the child romped with Coco, Mrs. Chambers sat on the edge of the porch and watched her granddaughter.

After ten minutes of silence, Kate said, "I would have made a terrible wife for Rob. You have to admit that."

Mrs. Chambers said nothing for almost a

minute before she nodded. "I do, but you hurt him, Kate." She swiveled to make eye contact. "I can't forgive how deeply you hurt him, how much you embarrassed him before everyone in town." Her voice hardened.

"If we'd gotten married, I would have hurt him more."

Rob's mother didn't answer, but her posture relaxed a little. She and Kate watched Lora, listened to the childish giggles as they floated on the warm spring breeze, blending with the scent of apple and pear blossoms. But Mrs. Chambers didn't say another word until she stood and called, "Say goodbye to the puppy, Lora. Time to go home."

Not a brilliant success, but Mrs. Chambers hadn't glared at her. Kate would count that as a positive.

When the weekly Silver Lake *Sentinel* came out on Thursday morning, Kate thumbed through the ten pages as she drank her coffee. When she was in high school and over summer vacations, she'd spent hours working on the little paper. It had improved a great deal since she'd been a go-fer or written articles or helped with setup.

On the front page were stories about the fire department fund-raiser, the April school board meeting and plans for the town festival in July. News from the surrounding towns and church and wedding announcements filled the next pages. On pages eight and nine was athletic news.

Classified ads took up the last page. One of them had a thick, black border around it. "Wanted," Kate read. "Reporter for the *Sentinel*. Part-time. Good hours." The job Mrs. Watkins had mentioned. If she was going to be in town for a few months, working for the paper would be fun. Going back to her roots. Using her experience.

Foolish speculation. They'd want someone who'd be around for six or seven months or a year. And she still had to take care of Abby.

But the ad stated, "Good hours."

Friday morning Kate still considered the ad. Abby had allowed Kate to help her into a sweat suit and sneakers, to comb her hair and apply a little makeup. While she tied her sister's shoes, Kate said, "What would you think about my getting a job or volunteering someplace for a few days a week? You don't need me around that much."

"I don't need you around at all, but the doctor insisted." Abby pushed herself to her feet. "Go ahead. From that car you drive, I can tell you need to earn some money."

Yes, she did, but she hated that her lack of funds was so obvious.

Abby planned to spend a few hours on the back porch. For that reason, Kate descended the stairs in front of her.

"You don't really have to do that," Abby complained. "I've gone down the stairs ten or twelve times without falling." But she clenched the rail in her left hand and put both feet on each step before stepping down again.

Didn't look like the action of a confident woman.

"I don't mind." Oddly, Kate didn't. Abby had regained a lot of strength although she still babied her arm. She'd been downstairs for all her meals for three days and even spent an hour on the porch the previous evening while Kate and Brooke watered the geraniums and broke off dead flowers.

But she still protected her arm and clenched her teeth against pain.

After Abby settled in a chair with her book, Kate checked the condition of a beautiful mix of red and white impatiens planted in a barrel next to the side porch.

"How're you doing?"

Kate turned to see Rob kneeling on the porch in front of Abby. He wore khakis with a deep blue polo shirt that drew out the color of his eyes. "I looked out my window and saw you ensconced over here," he said to Abby. "It's good to see you up."

"She's been doing great." Kate emptied the watering can on the impatiens and wished she'd put on something nicer than her white shorts and Miami Dolphins T-shirt.

"Abby comes downstairs for meals now."

"Oh, for Pete's sake, I'm not a ninety-year-old invalid you have to fuss about." She put a hand on Rob's shoulder. "I'm doing well. Thanks for coming over. Thanks for making the pulley."

Kate opened her mouth to tell Rob how well the pulley worked but snapped it shut. Abby would probably consider that fussing, too. Instead she said, "Why don't you sit down and relax for a few minutes, Rob. I'll get some coffee and a few of the cookies Mrs. Oglesby brought by yesterday."

"Coffee would be great. Black." Rob settled in the chair next to Abby. "Don't have much time. I expect a conference call in fifteen minutes."

Kate watched them from the window over the sink and envied the camaraderie between the two. They looked like old friends. With Abby, Rob's jaw relaxed and the wary expression disappeared from his eyes while Abby actually smiled. After chatting for a few minutes, Abby said something that made Rob lean forward and ask a question. Then he stood. "I'll help Kate bring the coffee," she heard him say.

When he entered the kitchen, he leaned his elbows on the white tiles of the breakfast bar and stared at her across that expanse. "Abby says you're looking for a job in Silver Lake. Does that mean you're planning to stay?"

She couldn't read his face but his voice held a harsh, demanding tone.

After taking three mugs from the shelf, she filled each and considered her answer. "I am looking for a job here, something to keep me busy for a few weeks and make a little money, but I don't plan to stay after Abby's recovered."

This time she could read his expression. Relief, pure and simple.

"Does it matter to you? If I stay or if I leave?"

"Not a bit." He took two mugs and headed out the door, shoving it open with his elbow.

But it did. She didn't need to be a crack investigative reporter to recognize that Rob cared greatly whether or not she stayed or left.

And he favored her departure, most likely as soon as possible.

* * *

That afternoon, Kate settled in the kitchen chair she'd placed in front of her computer. She hadn't checked her e-mail in a month, not since she left Florida. Did she really want to read it? She couldn't imagine who might write her.

To her surprise, there were twenty-five unread messages. After clearing out the few pieces of junk her SPAM filter had missed, she started reading. The first few messages said "Keep in touch" in various ways, which she really appreciated. One suggested she write an acquaintance about a position. Below her level, of course, but it was a start. Probably the best she could expect at this time.

A truly brave friend said she'd write a reference. Several more gave suggestions and one or two added definite leads for jobs. Oh, the positions were in Wyoming and New Mexico and other states far from Florida, but they were possibilities.

She shook her head, unhappy that she'd given up on her friends but overjoyed they hadn't given up on her. Feeling better than she had in months, she saved the information on her stick drive and would print it later.

Then she pulled up her résumé and started to work on it. Impressive until a year ago when she quit her job with the congressman. That was followed by a job in a department store, another in a temp agency and a few weeks as a waitress before she came home.

She'd sold the condo and had been living off the interest of that investment and the tiny salaries of those jobs. She had to find another job or she'd have to dip further into her savings. She'd better start now.

So why, when she'd begun looking to the future and had some good leads, did the job at the newspaper kept popping up in her thoughts? She'd be here for only a few more weeks. But as Abby required less and less care, neither did Kate want to spend the entire time writing on a computer in her bedroom, walking Coco or watering the geraniums.

She hadn't always been this indecisive and found it a very unattractive trait. All she had to do was outgrow one fault and another turned up, one even less appealing than the other.

With a determined tapping, she brought her résumé up to date, saved it and sat back.

An accomplishment she could check off her list. If she had one.

Chapter Nine

"I'm Kate Wallace. I'm here about the part-time job in the paper."

The receptionist in the newspaper office, a young woman in jeans and a T-shirt, stared at Kate through round, metal-rimmed glasses. A sign on the desk said Lilibeth Gano.

"Do you have an appointment?"

Woops. Kate hadn't even thought about calling to schedule a time. Had she believed everyone would welcome her and hire her because she was the wonderful Kate Wallace? Although Mrs. Watkins had acted so enthusiastic, she shouldn't have assumed anything. She should have made an appointment.

"No, I saw the ad and chatted with the editor."

"Okay." The girl tapped on the desk with a

pencil. "Miss Ellie is interviewing for that. I'll see if she has time to see you." She picked up a receiver and punched a number in the keypad. "Someone here for an interview," she said. After a moment, she hung up.

"She'll see you in a moment." She gestured toward a narrow bench against the wall.

Different from what she was used to, but wasn't the idea that, as a mature adult, she didn't have to be so judgmental and pretentious? Were those traits she'd have to struggle against for the rest of her life? Surely with effort and grace, she could overcome both.

Maybe working at the *Sentinel* again would help her decide what was important in life. Could be she'd enjoy writing again, and it would be great to have something to put on that résumé other than the series of jobs she'd held in the past year. Of course, the job was part-time, and she bet the salary was less than half of what she'd been earning in Miami. She'd have to do better to survive. She'd have to find a place to live.

But her sister couldn't kick her out because Kate didn't live in *Abby's* house. It belonged to her, too. Maybe she could find another part of *her* house to live in if she decided to stay in Silver Lake.

Except, of course, she wouldn't do that, couldn't do that. This was a temporary job. She had to look to the future and hope someone would hire her full-time before she went completely broke instead of only partially broke.

After a few minutes, she heard footsteps from the back of the office, the loud tapping of high heels down a wooden hallway, and Mrs. Watkins strode through the arch into the waiting area. When she saw Kate, she threw her arms into the air. "Kate, so glad you're here," she exclaimed. "Are you really here to talk about the part-time position?"

When Kate stood and nodded, Mrs. Watkins grabbed her arm. "Come back to my office to talk about it." She tugged Kate down the hall. "Not that I need to know more. You're my top choice, but I imagine you'd like a job description."

Once inside the office, Mrs. Watkins pushed Kate into an upholstered chair in front of the scarred wooden desk and settled into one next to her.

"Mrs. Watkins, I'd love to work here, but I'll be in town for only a few more weeks, six at the most. Don't you need someone more permanent?"

"Permanent, shermament." She swept a hand in front of her, her large diamond ring glittering in the fluorescent light. "The job doesn't pay much. People who make this little money are constantly moving on. If you leave…"

"Not 'if,' Mrs. Watkins. When I leave."

"Kate." She leaned forward. "I know your work. I taught you. I read everything you wrote when you were at the newspaper in Houston. You're the one I want to hire for as much time as you can give me." She leaned back in the chair and crossed her legs. "Now, why don't you call me Ellie. Everyone does. I'm no longer your teacher."

"Oh, I can't do that." Kate grinned at the thought. "You were my teacher. You'll always be Mrs. Watkins to me."

She sighed dramatically. "Okay, if that's what you want." She picked up a folder from the desk. "The job is for twenty hours a week. I assign stories, but, other than having to cover certain events, the hours are flexible. I know you need to take care of you sister, which, because I know Abby well, can't be easy." She shook her head, the mountain of pale gold hair shifting slightly.

"She's my sister."

What surprised Kate was first that she'd said that and, second, that she did feel that way—almost. Feeling an odd emotional response to her answer, she added quickly, "And the pay?"

"Well, you're right there at the top of our reporters' salaries, with your experience, which means you may be able to eat but it's a good thing you don't have to pay rent."

When she named the amount Kate would earn per hour, Kate burst out in laughter. Then she glanced at Mrs. Watkins's face. "Oh, I'm sorry. You're serious."

"Wish I could pay more, but a small-town newspaper doesn't make much." She drummed her fingers on the arm of the chair. "When Arnold bought this for me when I retired from teaching, he knew running a newspaper was my dream." She shook her head. "I love it, but keeping a small-town newspaper afloat isn't easy. I have to cut corners everywhere. I know the salary's not even close to what you made before."

About ten percent of what she'd been living on in Florida, but it was a job in a newspaper with good hours. Where else would she find something in Silver Lake that paid more for part-time and that she'd enjoy that much? "I'll take it."

* * *

Kate picked up the phone. "Silver Lake *Sentinel.*" She grabbed a pencil and began taking notes about the May Festival at the community center.

Her desk was shoved into what must have been a storeroom or a mop closet at some time. No ceiling, no window outside and little privacy. The desk lamp spread a halo of light that didn't quite reach the walls. Beneath the desk, Coco snored.

Yes, the office was tiny, but she had a phone and a computer with a printer, everything she required. Mrs. Watkins had given her the choice of working here or at home and she'd chosen this because Kate needed to get out of the house as much as she needed the money.

Her first story, about the city council meeting in Valley Center fifteen miles to the north, had appeared in last week's issue of the *Sentinel.* The byline had pleased her nearly as much as any she'd had. It made her feel as if she were on her way back. She felt good and her days were filled with whispered prayers of thanksgiving.

With Coco curled up at her feet at night, Kate was sleeping deeply, satisfied with life for the first time in a long time. Perhaps the accumulated stress of years had fallen away from her or perhaps the long, peaceful nights had helped her catch up with the sleep deprivation. Whatever the reason, she felt invigorated and full of energy.

Last night, Marta Elisa had slept over with Brooke. Kate had put sleeping bags on the side porch on the opposite side of the house from Abby's windows.

Lora had come over with her grandmother a few afternoons to play with the puppy, but Rob hadn't stepped out of his house as far as Kate knew. She'd caught a glimpse of him at church but he'd slipped out during the closing hymn. That quick escape left her with a strange and completely unwanted sense of disappointment, which she tried, unsuccessfully, to shake off.

She glanced at the calendar on her desk. This afternoon, she and Coco would drive out to the lake where she'd interview the operator of the boat dock about Friday evening's church picnic and worship service at Silver Lake.

Maybe Rob would be there. But as soon as the thought popped into her head, she chased it away. She had no idea how she'd react if Rob were there. A friendly "Hello" from him? A quick smile or an even faster retreat? She wouldn't know until she saw him.

* * *

Rob hated being closed in this office, hunched over a computer. Usually he did that because he had projects due, but this week he'd had another reason, a blonde who lived only a few yards away.

He stood, shoving the chair backward to hit the wall behind him with a thud. He took a few steps toward the French door and looked out.

He'd carefully avoided Kate since the morning Abby told him—and Kate had confirmed—that she planned to get a job. Here. In Silver Lake.

When Abby passed that information along, he'd felt joy and hope, immediate but frightening in intensity.

How could he hope for even a second that Kate would stay here in Silver Lake? He didn't want to see her, attempted to ignore the fact that she was less than a football field away. Her proximity was too dangerous. She made him care a little, come alive a bit, remember he was still a man. Kate was prying his shell open. He didn't want that.

He refused to allow even the slightest crack in the wall he'd built around his emotions after Junie's diagnosis of her cancer. With the sheer power of his will, he guarded that barricade because it allowed him to function but not to feel.

His life, with all the barrier building involved, would've been much easier if Kate had never come home again.

He sat down to study his drawing for the new medical center on his monitor. After checking the size of the lab against state requirements, he pushed the chair away from the desk again leaned back to look at the ceiling. White and flat and boring. Just like his life.

Yeah, his life was monotonous. He was dull and uninteresting. All he did was work, play with Lora, eat with his mother and work more, stuck in this room.

He hadn't always been like this. When he was a kid, he'd played sports, had friends, done things. After he'd married Junie, they'd gone camping, white-water rafting. After Lora was born, they'd still camped. They'd gone out with friends or had friends over. They did stuff.

No, he hadn't always been this boring. For years he had a motorcycle he'd loved to ride with Kate and, later, with Junie hanging on to the back. He'd even raced it in high school.

He hadn't spent his entire life sitting at a

desk and pretending to live. Years ago, he hadn't merely existed, only gone through the motions of life because he had a daughter he loved and had to care for.

Didn't she deserve more than a robot for a father?

Didn't *he* deserve a better life? A real life?

With another shove against the desk, he stood and strode toward the French doors to the backyard. His mother's apartment took up most of the old garage, but he'd built a small storage space on the east side.

Once at the door to the storage room, he turned the knob, pulled the door open and reached for the chain of the overhead bulb. After he gave it a quick tug, a glow filled the small area illuminating motes of dust that floated around him. The space smelled musty and unused.

In the middle of the area stood his hog. He moved toward it and ran his hand down the handlebar. A light coating of grit covered it, rough against his fingers, but the black paint and silver trim shone. His mother must have cleaned it a few times in the past two years. Bless her.

He could tell that something had built a nest under the seat because recently hatched gecko eggs covered the floor. The whole mess looked a lot like his life felt—old and forgotten but, fortunately, without the broken eggs.

The last thought made him smile a little.

Maybe there was hope for him after all.

"Rob, are you all right?"

He turned to see his mother standing in the doorway. Her voice held a note of concern. Knowing how he hated her to worry about him, she attempted to disguise it.

"Mom, I'm fine. I just got started thinking about the motorcycle. Decided to come out and see…" He didn't know what he'd come out to see. That it was still there? With the big lock on the door, how could it have escaped on its own?

Maybe to see if it really did exist or maybe to remind himself that as a young, untroubled kid, he'd ridden it around the county feeling free, taking curves too fast. He closed his eyes, remembering how he'd raced it at the local raceway at speeds he couldn't imagine doing now, risking everything for the few trophies he'd won and his mother still kept someplace.

Had he thought that seeing the cycle would remind him that he had once been young and carefree? That the fearless kid had really existed and maybe still did? But he didn't think so. The kid had disappeared long before he'd locked the machine back here.

"I'm fine," he said.

"Are you here looking at that thing because she's back?" She pointed in the direction of Kate's house.

If there were another topic he'd prefer not to discuss with his mother, he didn't know what it was. "I'm fine," he repeated.

She nodded and turned away.

He knew he hadn't convinced her of anything. He hadn't convinced himself, either, except that a little of his sense of humor had returned. That had to be a good thing.

Rinsing out her glass in the kitchen, Kate studied the night sky outside the window where a waxing crescent moon glowed. As it glided between two clouds, a lacy design feathered the lunar edges.

Over the hedge between the houses and across a bit of the Dkaneys' backyard, Kate caught a glimpse of Rob's head through a downstairs window in his house. If she scooted a little to the right and stood on tiptoe, she could probably see more. Was he in the kitchen or his office or another room?

What would he be doing now? Working or

washing dishes? Oddly Kate found doing housework very attractive in a man. She guessed most women did. An old Texas adage stated, "A man's never been shot while washing dishes." Probably true.

His head disappeared for a moment. Leaning farther to the right and stretching up, she could see more of the window but still caught no view of Rob.

"What are you doing?"

Kate froze, straightened, then turned slowly, dropping to her normal height. Brooke stood only a few inches from her, bobbing around in an effort to follow her aunt's gaze.

Her niece had caught her. Again.

"Nothing," Kate mumbled, feeling a little guilty about the fib, but she wouldn't feel comfortable saying, "I'm trying to catch a glimpse of the man I left behind but still find very attractive and wonder if he feels that way about me but doubt it because he acts like I'm not around."

No, she could never say that so she said, "Getting a glass of water." She looked down to find her glass overflowing and the sink half full of water. With a flick of her wrist, she turned off the faucet and poured half of the water down the drain.

Brooke leaned against the counter, taking in every embarrassing move her aunt made. "Are you in love with Mr. Chambers?"

"Of course not." That was true. She *had* loved him as a young woman. She liked him now. She found him very attractive now, but that—and the staring out the window to get a glimpse at him—didn't mean she really, really liked him.

Did it?

"Then why were you almost falling over to look in the window of his house?"

"I wasn't exactly…" But she had been and Brooke had seen it. Foolish to deny it.

"That's not the way I look at my friends." Brooke paused and thought for a moment. "That's how I'd look at Sammy Newton, wiggling around and standing on tiptoes to get a really good look at him."

"Who's Sammy Newton?"

"He's the cutest boy in fourth grade. If it wasn't rude and probably illegal, I'd try to look in his window, too." She grinned. "That's how you look at the Chambers's house, Aunt Kate, like you're interested in someone there, really, really interested."

Abby's bell tinkled from upstairs, a sound that filled Kate with relief, a new reaction to that usually dreaded summons. "I have to go up and check on your mother. Maybe she'll want to come down and watch television with us."

Kate hurried to the hall and headed upstairs. Behind her, she could feel Brooke's eyes watching her. An escape, but she had the terrible feeling her niece wouldn't let her run away so easily from every question she asked. Brooke wasn't through asking or noticing how Kate looked at Rob.

Brooke's questions had no answers. They reminded Kate that she still felt something for Rob or perhaps she felt something new for *this* Rob or maybe she had feelings left over for the *old* Rob.

She didn't want to care about anyone here. The plan had been to dash in and find a new job while she nursed her sister and not to spend any money.

Being attracted to Rob had no part in that strategy.

Friday, Kate-the-sister became Kate-the-reporter. She had to cover preparations for the library literacy fund-raiser for the *Sentinel* before she raced home to get Abby lunch. After that, she attended a city council meeting in San Saba. Finally she came home and got ready for the church picnic.

She hated to admit she was excited about the evening. She'd attended parties in embassies and receptions for national and international leaders, many in the giddy and high-powered atmosphere of D.C. and several in London, but she'd rarely felt the tingle of anticipation that filled her now.

She feared she knew the reason for her feelings but pushed the notion back, hard, into the area of her brain where she kept all those ideas and concepts she didn't want to explore. Ever.

"Are you sure you don't want to come with us tonight?" she asked her sister. "If you get tired, I'll bring you back home."

Abby sat at the kitchen table eating a bowl of ice cream, not looking nearly as pale as she had after her first trip downstairs weeks earlier. "No, you go ahead." She glanced at Kate for a moment before she dropped her gaze back to the fascinating view of cookie-dough ice cream. "I don't want Brooke to miss anything. She's really looking forward to canoeing on the lake."

Kate almost dropped the glass of lemonade she had poured for her sister but placed it on the table before the accident happened. Her sister's statement constituted the first maternal expression she'd heard from Abby. Instead of asking, "What did you say?" Kate said, "Yes, she is. You're a good mother to think of that."

Probably the expected reaction, gauging by Abby's raised eyebrow.

One bit of knowledge Kate had not pushed into that overstuffed corner of her brain was that she and Abby were no closer than they had been a few weeks ago, than they had been when she left Silver Lake. Kate had no idea what to do about the chasm separating them. She prayed, she read a book on getting along with difficult people, she'd attempted to talk with Abby, putting forth interesting questions which her sister ignored. With all that, nothing changed.

For a moment, she considered sitting down and apologizing to Abby for everything she'd done to hurt her, most especially for the act that had given Abby a reason to dislike her, and beg forgiveness. She would do all that to heal the rift, to build a good relationship with her only sister. But before she could, the phone rang. This time, she hadn't wanted the interruption.

"I'll get it." Abby stood and reached toward the receiver.

While she talked to someone from the bank, Kate cleared the table and knew she'd have to make time, a definite time, for that apology, as painful as it would be for both of them.

But now she had to get ready for the church picnic.

Chapter Ten

Kate drove slowly, the car bouncing along the rutted road of Silver Lake Park.

"Do you see a place to park?" She leaned forward to stare at the solid line of cars pulled in on both sides of the road.

Finally Kate had to settle for a place almost two blocks from the picnic area. When she turned off the engine, Brooke sprang from the car.

"I'll meet you at the barbecue pit." Brooke's voice trailed behind her as she sprinted up the rutted road, her hair streaming behind her.

"Brooke," Kate shouted but the child had raced beyond the sound of her voice. She'd have to lug everything herself. She hit the button to open the trunk. With a groan, the lid of what Brooke called "that hideous car" slowly lifted.

She picked up the large basket of sandwiches and box of cookies she'd brought, slung the cooler over her shoulder, slammed the trunk closed and took off toward the laughter and noise.

As Rob walked through the crowd of church members, their friends and families, Lora bounced on his shoulder. She wiggled and crowed and waved to everyone. They all waved back to her and smiled.

Mom had hurried her pies and fried chicken to the long table where the women were setting up and left him here. Normally that wouldn't be a problem, but tonight one question repeated in his brain.

Would Kate be here?

He stopped and looked around, not in an effort to find Kate but to find someone, anyone, who would keep his mind off her.

"Rob, how wonderful to see you and your precious daughter." Mrs. Watkins stopped in front of him and lifted the jeweled fingers of her right hand to pat Lora's cheek. "Aren't you the cutest little doll."

"Thank you, Mrs. Watkins. Nice to see you here."

"I don't know why all my former students insist on calling me Mrs. Watkins."

"Because you were our teacher."

"That's exactly what Kate said." She patted his arm. "Do you know Kate Wallace is working for me now? Doing a terrific job." She lifted her head and began to search the crowd. "Weren't you two in school together? I'll see if I can find her. I'm sure she'd love to tell you herself."

Using Mrs. Watkins as a refuge from Kate hadn't worked out as well as he'd hoped. He glanced above his former teacher's head, looking to find a safe spot, maybe over there where several men gathered by the barbecue pit. That looked like a masculine zone. Hot coals and manly talk.

"Weren't you and Kate elected Mr. and Mrs. Silver Lake High School in the same year? After all the time I taught it's hard for me to remember." Then she closed her eyes until the long, dark lashes fluttered. Then her eyes flew open, as if she suddenly recalled everything. "Oh, yes, you were *very* good friends, but then she left and you married Junie and had this lovely child." She sighed. "So darling." With a wave of her ruby-colored nails, she took off toward a group of women arranging food on the picnic tables.

"Hey, Rob." The men, many of whom he'd played football with, greeted him as he approached the barbecue pit. "Good to see you."

"We're trying to figure out the best way to get this fire going. I want to use the old-fashioned way. You know, kindling and newspaper," Reverend Moreno explained.

Rob listened to the argument for a few minutes before he noticed Brooke hovering around the edge of the group.

When she saw him, she hurried over and whispered, "Have you seen Aunt Kate?"

Probably not a good idea to tell her he'd been avoiding Kate. He shook his head.

"I was supposed to meet her here," Brooke said. "But I saw a couple of friends and started talking to them. Now I can't find her."

"Don't worry. She'll find you."

The frown of a longtime worrier covered Brooke's features. "I don't want her to be unhappy because I ran off."

On his shoulders, Lora began to wiggle. "Hello," she said to Brooke. "Puppy's friend." Brooke's frown disappeared to be replaced by a grin.

"Have you tried the tables over there, where the food is?" He waved in that direction.

When Lora wiggled more and held her

hands out, Rob swung her off his shoulders, put her on the ground and took her hand. Lora had a different idea. She reached her arms toward Brooke. "Hello."

"Hi, Lora." Brooke leaned down and held a hand out. "Do you want to come with me?" When Lora took her hand, Brooke glanced up. "Is it okay for me to take her for a while?"

"Sure. Make sure she doesn't get away from you. She's fast." He watched Lora toddle off, feeling alone and almost vulnerable without his shield.

His shield? When had he started thinking of his daughter as his shield? And against what?

His mother would say against life, but she'd always been overly dramatic.

At that moment Kate strode toward the barbecue pit. Yes, he *did* know what he'd planned to use Lora to guard against. Kate. He took a couple of steps back until the sharp leaf of an agarita bush pricked him. Fortunately, by that time he found himself behind several stumpy mesquites and a big tooth maple. He didn't think she'd seen him, but he heard her ask in frustration if anyone had seen Brooke.

Alone in the isolation afforded by the small copse, he watched her face and the expressions that played across it. With the added vibrancy of her emotions and the maturity her years away from Silver Lake had added to her features, she was more beautiful than she'd been as Miss Mesa County.

Which was exactly why he was acting like such a spineless coward.

He turned to his right to see Brooke and his daughter. When Rob reached Brooke, he took Lora's hand and told Brooke where to find her aunt.

After dinner as they prepared the worship center for the vesper service, he noticed Brooke and Sara's foster daughter talking very seriously by the edge of the clearing. There was a lot of giggling going on. Probably hatching a plot or a practical joke against some poor young man. He grinned. What trick would they play on the unfortunate kid?

Finished with the setup, he walked carefully between other blankets toward the red blanket where his mother and Lora waited for him.

And almost stepped on Kate's hand.

Seated with Brooke and Sara with her four children, Kate sat at the edge of the very crowded blanket.

"Ladies," he said as he moved past them.

The girls laughed and punched each other.

Had one of them told a joke or were they just silly? Would Lora be that way when she was their age? Probably, which meant a tough time ahead because he had no idea what he'd do with a giggling nine-year-old.

As he settled next to his mother and took Lora in his arms, he allowed himself one more furtive glance at Kate. When he did, he discovered two pairs of eyes looking back at him—Brooke's and her friend's.

With Brooke snuggled up to her side, Kate thought how nice it was to have family, to sit with them at worship, to spend time and build memories.

The worship area faced the lake. The sun had set and a full moon drifted across the horizon, leaving a silver trail in the water. After Reverend Moreno called them together, Mrs. Oglesby read the verses from the eighth Psalm, "O Lord, our Lord, how majestic is your name in all the earth! You have set your glory above the heavens… When I consider your heavens, the work of your fingers, the moon and the stars, which you have set in place…what is man that you are mindful of him, the son of man that you care for him?… O Lord, our Lord, how majestic is your name in all the earth!"

At her side, Kate felt Brooke shiver. She glanced down to find her niece studying the sky and the reflection of the moon in the water.

"Now I understand those words," Brooke whispered and gestured toward the reflection of the moon on the lake.

"What do you mean?"

"How could the one who created all this still care for us?" She paused. "But He does. Isn't that a miracle?"

Kate nodded, deeply touched by the depth of Brooke's faith and understanding. "You have set your glory above the heavens," she whispered.

"'When I consider your heavens,'" Brooke whispered as she studied the silvery shimmering in the water. "Isn't God's creation beautiful?"

For a moment, Kate felt a warmth as love and hope spread through her. She pulled Brooke closer with a hug.

"Thank you for bringing me," Brooke whispered.

After a hymn and a short meditation, the minister gave a benediction. With that, almost everyone stood and headed toward the lake, some to swim, others to take one of the canoes out on the water. Others went to the volleyball courts or the basketball goals.

Rob sat with his mother, Lora sleeping between them. As Kate watched, Marta Elisa approached him to ask him something. After a short conversation, he stood and followed her.

"Aunt Kate." Brooke stood a few feet from her. "Would you take me on a canoe ride?"

Kate didn't want to go. More than anything, she wanted to stay here, to meditate and put the hope that had filled her into her life, to allow it to lead to her future.

"Aunt Kate?" Brooke repeated.

But it didn't look as if this were the time or place for that. "I haven't been in a canoe for years, not since I was in high school."

For a second, a look of panic covered Brooke's face, then she said, "How hard can it be? Besides—" she gestured toward the crowd around the lake "—if we have a problem, the water is shallow and lots of people are close. What could go wrong?"

Probably nothing, and paddling with Brooke around the lake would be fun. "Life jackets?" she asked.

"Of course."

The moon shone brightly and beautifully off the lake. Kate wanted to walk slowly to enjoy it, but Brooke had grabbed her arm and was pulling her down the slope toward the dock.

"What's the hurry?" Kate asked.

"We…we…we, um, want to be sure to get a canoe."

Why was her niece acting so oddly?

As they approached the water, Kate noticed Rob helping Marta Elisa into an aluminum canoe. When he sat in the back of the canoe, he picked up a paddle and nodded to Marta Elisa, but the girl didn't let go of the line tied to the dock. Although the canoe pulled hard away from the dock, Marta Elisa groaned but continued to hold the rope tightly.

"Look, Rob and your friend are going to take a ride." Kate pointed.

"Uh-huh. Look at that."

Brooke's voice held a note of—what? Uncertainty? Discomfort? Apprehension? Kate couldn't interpret it, but something strange was going on in the child's mind.

"Can we go with Rob and Marta?"

So that's what it was. Brooke and Marta had set up some sort of scheme to get her together with Rob. She stopped on the edge of the dock and watched Rob, who seemed to be unaware of what the girls had plotted, and Marta, who grimaced from the strain of holding on to the dock.

"There's an empty rowboat." Kate pointed

to the other side of the pier. "We could use that."

"No, I don't like them." Brooke paused as if searching for words. "They're clunky and slow."

"We could each take an oar…"

"But…but…but," Brooke sputtered. "I *really* want to take a canoe ride. Let's go with Rob and Marta."

What difference would it make? Marta and Brooke would be with them so they wouldn't be alone. Besides, she liked canoes better than rowboats, too. "Okay."

"All right!" Brooke raised her clenched fists and boogied in victory. "Let's go." She took a few steps toward the canoe. "May we join you?" she asked Marta and Rob.

His expression neutral, Rob sat at the back of the canoe, balancing the paddle in his hands and obviously ready to go.

"Is there enough room for all of us?" Kate asked.

"Yes," Brooke said. "It's a fifteen-foot boat with a capacity for six hundred pounds." She chuckled self-consciously. "I think we're way under that."

Odder and odder. How did Brooke know about the weight limit for this canoe? She started to ask but Brooke hurried her toward the edge of the dock. Careful to keep the canoe balanced, Kate lowered herself into the front seat while Brooke joined Marta in the middle.

"Ready?" Marta asked as she dropped the rope and pushed off.

As the motion took them away from land and a few feet toward the center of the lake, Kate dipped her paddle in the water to lessen the sideways rocking of the light boat. "Brooke, did you get a life jacket?"

"No, Aunt Kate. I forgot." She giggled. "We'll go get them."

With that, the two girls stood and jumped from the canoe, one on each side. Even as she heard the sound of splashing as they headed for the shore, she had to shift her weight and struggle to keep the canoe from tipping over.

"Brooke," she shouted as she turned to look behind her once the canoe stabilized. By this time, the girls had swum toward the shore and stood in the shallow water, laughing.

And she was alone in the canoe with Rob.

After a few seconds, while the meaning of what had happened soaked in, he said, "I think we've been set up."

How did he feel about that? She glanced at him over her shoulder. Because his expression and his voice were unreadable, Kate had no idea what he thought. She felt pure embarrassment and anger. How could Brooke have done this?

Well, her niece *had* seen Kate attempting to look into the Chambers's house the other night and the earlier time when she'd watched him building the ramp. If Brooke had set this up because she'd noticed Kate's interest in Rob, did this mean Brooke had seen Rob show interest in her?

Probably not. These were young girls having fun, playing a prank. She guessed they had no idea how awkward this would be for the two adults left in the canoe.

Then she heard Rob chuckle from the back and began to laugh with him. "They sure put one over on us," he said.

"I didn't expect it at all." She dipped her paddle in the water and watched it glide through the silvery surface. "Do you want to go back?"

"We're out here. Let's enjoy this beautiful night." After nearly a minute, he added, "Why don't you stop paddling? I can handle it. You don't weigh enough to make this difficult."

She laid the paddle in the bottom of the boat, then, making sure she didn't move too quickly and capsize the canoe, she turned around on the seat to face Rob.

Feathering the water, he pulled the boat farther from the shore, easily moving the canoe along. His broad shoulders stood out against the glimmering light of the moon.

"Rob." A shot of courage filled her after he'd paddled for a few more strokes, but she couldn't get any more words out. She reminded herself that her entire professional life had been spent asking and answering questions no one wanted to hear. Of course, look where that had landed her. Back home where she'd started.

But she knew Rob wouldn't be the one to bring up what she wanted to know. She'd left him, after all. If she'd learned anything over the past years, it was that if she wanted to know something, she had to ask.

Taking a deep breath, she said, "Do you think we have a future together?"

His paddle skipped in the water, sprinkling drops of the clear, cold water into the canoe, but he didn't speak.

"Is there still anything between us? Is there any chance we can build a new relationship?" she asked. "Would you even want to?"

She didn't think he was going to answer. He

kept going, dipping the paddle in and out of the water, as they moved farther and farther from the fire on the shore.

"I don't know."

That was it. That was all he said. She waited and wished she knew what he was feeling, but he still wore the expression that gave nothing away. When they'd dated, she could always tell what he felt, from seldom-seen anger that flashed in his eyes to the happiness that usually lit up his face and eyes. Not now.

After nearly a minute, he rested the paddle across his knees and allowed the canoe to rock. "I don't want to feel anything for you. I loved Junie very much, and I thought I'd forgotten you." He stopped talking and studied her expression. "But I see you and remember how much I used to love you."

"Do you feel anything now?" She kept her voice calm and patient.

He shrugged. "We're different now, both of us. I don't know if anything between people who haven't seen each other in years could be real, not after only a few weeks together."

She nodded.

"You have to understand one thing clearly. I don't want to care about you." He paused and looked at the sky. "I don't want to care about you, but, no matter how I fight it, I think about you."

"Maybe we need to start over, pretend we didn't know each other. If we do that… Well, we could try."

"Why, Kate?" He picked up the paddle and cut into the water with determined strokes to turn them back toward the shore. "Even though you have a job here, you're leaving in a few weeks. Why would you want to start over again?"

"I left a lot unfinished here."

"Yes, you did, and I refuse to be a project you can finish before you run off again."

"I understand." She struggled with her words. "I'd like to see if you and I have something, anything, together. I don't want to leave and not know." She paused, again trying to read that closed-off expression, then whispered, "Maybe I don't want to leave."

As they neared the shore, Kate looked behind her. Already she could see the outline of people around the bonfire. "I'd like to know if there can be a spark, a flame, anything between us." She faced Rob and attempted to break through to him. "If not, if there's no future for us, we'll both know. We can call this part of our lives over."

"Kate, I closed the door on what was between us when I fell in love with Junie."

"You said you still think about me."

"But I don't want to. That says it all. I don't want to."

"Are you sure? Are you so sure that you're not willing to take a risk?"

"I don't take chances anymore. I outgrew that."

What could she say to convince him?

Nothing. She couldn't build a relationship by herself. Even if his words had left a small opening, his determined expression shut her out.

When they reached the dock, Rob jumped out, took the rope and tied it to the dock post. That completed, he reached down to help Kate out, not as a wish to touch her, Kate was sure, but because Rob was always a gentleman.

As he tugged her forward, she tripped on the warped boards and fell toward him. Releasing her hand, Rob grabbed her around the waist to steady her and pull her to her feet.

Feeling him so close, Kate couldn't help herself. She leaned into his chest, only for a moment, for a sense of his warmth and strength, for the nearness of Rob she'd missed for so many years and found.

Rob drew in a deep breath. "Kate, I don't want to do this." His voice was low and anguished. "I don't want this."

But instead of pushing her away, he folded his arms around her and laid his cheek against the top of her head.

"I keep telling myself I don't want to care for you, but I do." The words came as if they were being pulled from him. "Kate, I still want to be with you." He didn't say a word for a few heartbeats, only held her.

"All right," he said with a groan. "Whatever happens, wherever that goes, I'm ready to try again. The way I feel when I hold you...well, I don't know if I have a choice. I have to know if we can find something together."

She leaned back to look into his face where she read a great deal of uncertainty and a constrained happiness.

Constrained happiness was something she could work with, build on. "Whatever happens," she agreed. "Wherever this goes."

More than anything, she wanted Rob to kiss her, but a group of church youth giggled and joked on the beach only twenty yards away while Brooke was running across the dock toward them. Kate stepped away.

"This isn't over," he said.

The promise in his voice made her tingle with anticipation about the next time she'd be with Rob. She had her work cut out for her because the doubt in his expression presented a huge challenge.

Kate drove home a little after eleven o'clock with Brooke asleep in the passenger seat. While stopped at a light, Kate studied her niece. The child had changed in the past few weeks. She laughed, she talked and the lines between her eyes had faded. Oh, she still wasn't a normal nine-year-old, at least not in what Kate considered her less than expert opinion, but she seemed happier now.

After pulling the car into the driveway and shutting off the engine, she gently shook Brooke. "Wake up."

Brooke opened her eyes and stretched. "Oh, Aunt Kate. Thank you for taking me. That was the most wonderful time I've ever had." She smiled then reached across the front seat to hug Kate, a warm, loving hug. "Thank you."

Kate hugged her back, her heart expanding with a feeling that had been growing since she met her niece. "You're welcome, Brooke." After a last squeeze, she added, "I love you."

Brooke pulled back in surprise and blinked before she opened the door and slid out to run inside. As she watched the child's back disappear, Kate realized she'd frightened her niece. Well, all battles weren't won in a month, and she was glad she'd said the words. Brooke was family, a link, part of a chain that had broken when she left and, later, when her parents died. Forging those links again had become important to her.

That evening she lay in bed and considered all that had happened in the past few hours during one of the best nights of her life. Brooke had shared her faith. Rob had held her, suggesting there might be more for them. Maybe not the best time of her life to follow up on a relationship, but this was important. She'd make time. She'd stay here as long as necessary because Rob was worth it.

Kate turned over in bed, causing Coco to wake up and woof a few times. Reaching down to pet her, Kate glanced out the window. Although she couldn't see the moon, its shining light still streaked the sky.

She stood, careful not to disturb Coco again, and opened the window to lean out. She could see the corner of the Chambers's house. A breeze brought the fragrance of honeysuckle from the vines along the alleyway. Across that passage, she saw the roses growing in the Nortons' yard, their colors muted in the light of the moon.

Around her she could feel the town, warm and comfortable. Welcoming. She'd come home.

God had given her direction even when she hadn't been looking for it. Even when she hadn't been listening.

Well, she'd be listening from now on.

Chapter Eleven

"I told your mother I'd have made a terrible wife," Kate confessed as Rob pulled his sedan into a parking place in front of the Potter House, a restaurant in nearby Granite Falls. It was Tuesday, four days after the church picnic.

"You've always been honest, Kate." He grinned at her. "You're right. You would have made an awful wife."

She waited until he rounded the car and opened her door to speak. "You don't have to agree so strongly." She laughed. "You could disagree just a bit, to be polite."

Rob put his hand out to help her stand. "But I do agree. If we'd gotten married after we both finished school, it wouldn't have lasted."

Once she was out of the car, he dropped her hand and followed her toward the door. She ran her hand down the taupe slacks and silk shirt she wore, the same outfit she'd worn to church. Not that she had much choice. She could have bought a new outfit, but with her tight budget and her effort not to obsess over this date, she'd settled on the one nice outfit she'd brought with her.

On the other hand, Rob looked terrific as he opened the heavy wood door of the restaurant and allowed her to precede him. Just the right balance of casual and special in his open-necked blue dress shirt, dark blue slacks and tasseled loafers.

As the door closed behind them, a hostess in a long black dress led them to a round table and handed them each a menu. The tall windows that enclosed the dining room over-looked the lights of the small town. In the distance, she could see the lake.

"They have great steaks and seafood here." Rob had settled in the chair next to her and pulled it away, just a little. Not far, but enough to make a slight difference.

He still wasn't completely comfortable with the situation, Kate observed. Not that it took a brilliant, intuitive mind to notice that.

"You used to love salmon and fried shrimp. Do you still or do you have lobster tastes now?" he asked. Pleasant but not enthusiastic. Had the days between the picnic and this dinner given him time to reconsider pursuing a relationship?

"Not on my budget." Glancing out the window, she added, "Great view. New restaurant?" Why was she speaking in incomplete sentences?

"It was built about three years ago." He looked down at his menu. "I designed it." He tossed the words off as if they meant nothing.

She surveyed the room, noticing the beamed ceiling, the large stone fireplace and the interesting angles of the walls. All gave the restaurant the ambiance of an old building while the windows allowed a lovely panorama of the hill country, the Highland Lakes and Granite Falls below them.

"It's beautiful. Absolutely spectacular." She moved her glance to his face. "You must be very proud of this."

"Yeah." He nodded. A grin softened his face. "I am. Good food, great view and, well, my ideas."

Before she could say more, the waitress came for their order.

"All right," Kate said after she closed her menu and handed it to the waitress. "Why do you agree I would have been a terrible wife?"

"Because you didn't want to be a wife." Rob's fingers gripped the glass of water. "You wanted to go out into the world, to see what you could do with all your talent and drive. You needed to. I understood then, and I do now."

She nodded. "I tried, Rob. I loved you. I wanted to be a good wife."

"Not enough. Not back then."

For a few seconds, the air hummed with both regret and attraction. The question hung on the air between them: What about now?

But each ignored it. She didn't want to consider the question and she *knew* Rob didn't, either.

"Did I hurt you?" she asked.

"Of course." He raised his eyes to meet hers. "I think when you made that decision, it probably hurt you, too."

"That's the bad part, Rob. I didn't *make* a choice."

He raised an eyebrow.

"Instead I sort of *slid* into the decision without considering anyone else. It happened so gradually. I didn't realize I'd hurt you until I couldn't change things." She paused.

Knowing she had to be honest, she added, "No, that's not right. I knew I was going to hurt you, but I didn't want to change my life and come back here. I'm sorry."

"It was better for you, Kate. I know that. The hard part was that you preferred a newspaper to a person, to me." He held his hand up. "No, that's unfair. I love buildings and planning them, so I have an idea of how you felt. And for many years, I had something far better than buildings. Junie." He smiled, joy illuminating his entire face. "Junie and Lora. I've been blessed by them. I wouldn't have given them up for…for anything or anyone. So your decision worked well for all of us."

Accepting those words didn't feel good, but they were true. She had to get used to it. Rob had loved Junie deeply and probably still did. While she'd been running around in the circles of power, he'd been making a life for the two of them and creating another life, Lora.

She nodded. "You're right. Even though my career ended badly, I wouldn't have wanted to miss the excitement and the experience of my years in Houston and Florida." She smiled. "Which means we are two people who are glad we didn't get married. Although that may hurt our egos, it didn't break our hearts."

When he smiled back at her, the smile didn't quite reach the eyes but it was getting closer.

After dinner and a drive around the lake, Rob pulled in front of Kate's home at nearly midnight and turned off the engine. With a glance, he saw the house was dark except for a light on the back porch.

"I have to go through the yard," Kate said after he got out and went around to open her door. "Coco's back there. I'll need to take her in. When I do, you can watch her go up your ramp."

"Certain to be the highlight of the evening." He followed her toward the gate.

She glanced at him quickly, not smiling and maybe a little hurt.

"Just kidding."

Strange she'd react that way. Hadn't the years and her demanding jobs left her too tough to react to such a slight tease? Obviously not, so he added, "I enjoyed tonight. Good food. Good company."

"Thank you." She put her hand on his arm. "I enjoyed it, too."

She kept her fingers in place while they strolled toward the backyard, balancing herself as her thin heel sunk into the lawn. The moon covered the sky with silver light, which cast leafy shadows through the trees. Once when Kate stumbled, he reached his arm around her waist to steady her, then pulled it back when he realized how good holding her felt.

Getting to know each other better, finding out if anything could work out between them was harder than he'd thought. More painful and less fun. He was allowing Kate into territory he'd closed off. If he didn't watch out, that poor idiot—the young and trusting Rob he used to be—might turn up. That guy didn't stand a chance. That guy might still love Kate and wouldn't realize what was ahead when she left.

Because she *would* leave.

The thought reminded him that, in spite of the moon and the breeze and the romantic atmosphere, he couldn't trust Kate. In fact, there was very little he did trust anymore. He certainly couldn't trust a promise of forever with the woman he loved. He'd learned that the hard way. Twice. He didn't want to try for a third time.

A few steps inside the fence, he heard the rustling of Coco as she ambled across the grass and woofed. Kate kneeled. "Hello, Coco." She scratched behind the dog's ears. "Were you all right out here?"

As he and Kate stepped onto the porch, Coco trotted—well, as fast as she could trot—to the ramp and meandered up it.

"It works pretty well." He had to smile as the little dog walked across the porch to sit patiently by the back door.

"Thank you, Rob." Kate stood and leaned toward him, only a fraction of an inch, but the change in proximity was noticeable. When he didn't move toward her or hold a hand out, she stepped back.

Which, perversely, made him take a step toward Kate, narrowing the distance between them so he could catch the scent of her perfume and feel her warmth. Then, as he lowered his head, his eyes caught a movement in the kitchen window. When he pulled his gaze away from Kate's warm, pink lips, it met the eyes of a person standing inside.

He straightened and stepped away. "I think someone is watching us."

Kate turned toward the window. "Probably Brooke. She was so excited we were going out tonight."

When he realized how much he wanted to kiss Kate at that moment, longing warred with his common sense. Common sense didn't stand a chance.

"I think she's gone." With those words, he pulled Kate into his arms—warm, soft and beautiful Kate—and dropped his lips on hers.

She wrapped her arms around his neck and returned the kiss. When he finally realized how great the embrace felt, Rob pulled away. With his hands still on her back, he looked down at Kate's face. Her eyes were barely open, her expression a little dazed.

"Very nice," she whispered at the same time the lights in his backyard went on. "But I think your mother is waiting up for you." She stepped away.

He laughed. "She doesn't realize I'm over thirty and can go out without her waiting up for me."

But Kate didn't laugh. She looked at him with—what? Longing? Uncertainty? He couldn't tell.

Then Coco woofed impatiently. "I guess you'd better go," she said reluctantly.

"Fixin' to." He nodded. "Good night, Kate."

"Thank you for a wonderful time."

He turned and loped across the yard and out to his truck in the driveway, thankful that Coco had woofed and that his mother had been waiting up for him. If not, who knows what he might have said or promised or what emotion he might have given away because he realized how very drawn he was to the woman Kate had become.

After he parked the car in his driveway, he turned off the light his mother had so thoughtfully turned on for her son. Once inside the house, he had to face how much he'd enjoyed the kiss. No excuses. No pretending. No regrets. It had been great.

Of course, that could be because he hadn't kissed a woman in that way in years, not since before Junie's final illness. It could be that he missed the closeness he and Junie had shared, that he wanted to hold a woman again and it wouldn't make much difference who the woman was. It could be that he was lonely and needed to feel the presence of another human being.

Man oh man. Talk about lying to himself. He knew he'd kissed *Kate,* not just another human being. He'd kissed her as a man kisses a woman. He'd held her and known that the woman in his arms wasn't Junie, wasn't anyone else but Kate.

He locked the door behind him, acknowledging he still didn't know how to handle what had happened with Kate or how he felt about it.

But, if he had to give an opinion, he thought he was scared to death.

Friday morning, Abby had been settled into a chair on the porch. With Coco at her heels, Kate was able to wander through the old west wing of the house. This part, an ell that turned off from the downstairs parlor and upstairs bedroom wing, had been shut off years ago. In the late nineteenth century, their great-great-grandfather had added this section when his seventh child was born. He'd done a good job of matching the earlier Victorian style, both inside and out, but no one needed this much space now. It had been maintained well and cleaned regularly, but there was no furniture and, as far back as Kate remembered, no one had slept in this wing since she and Sara had camped here a couple of times in grade school.

She knew that on the first floor was a tiny parlor, a bathroom and two bedrooms. On the second were three more bedrooms. What could she do with the space? "We'd have to use the first floor so you can get out," she told Coco, who had settled on the tiles around the fireplace.

She opened the door from the parlor to the back porch. Coco's ramp was only a few yards away.

If she stayed in Silver Lake, could she live here?

It was private, but she'd still be close to Brooke, which was important to her. She could close off the door into the main parlor for privacy and make one of the bedrooms into a kitchen and dining area. The porch door would serve as a separate entry.

Standing in the hallway, she turned around to look into each room. Yes, it could work very well.

If she decided to stay here.

Maybe she'd call Rob after work and see if he'd give her some ideas.

What would he think if she called him? Would that be too forward of her?

When had she ever cared about being too forward?

She steepled her fingers to consider their relationship. After all, he hadn't called since their date three days earlier. Of course, he was probably busy, but did that mean he no longer wanted to explore their relationship? That he still believed she'd make a terrible wife?

Not, of course, that marriage was a topic of discussion between them or of the slightest bit of interest to either. No need for him to be frightened about that.

But there was that kiss. It hadn't been the kiss of old friends. It had been a kiss of two people who had cared for each other or might care for each other again if they allowed it, if they could get over the past and find out who they were now, who they were together.

Maybe she'd ask Sara to talk to Rob and…

She grinned and shook her head. She wasn't in high school anymore. They were adults. If she wanted to know how he felt, she'd ask him.

But right now, she wanted to talk to him about the possibilities and problems of making an apartment in this house for her. That was all.

"This would work out great for you, Kate." Later that afternoon, Rob held a pencil, clipboard and laser measuring device as he looked around the rooms Kate had shown him. "The best place to put a kitchen would be the little bedroom. It's closest to the plumbing in the bathroom." He pointed. "That change is about all it would take."

Yes, the remodel would be easy, but the idea of Kate deciding to live here, well, that wasn't as easy to accept.

"How expensive do you think it will be?"

"Not much. You can find good used appliances. It depends on how much you want to spend and how much furniture you need, but the remodel's easy." He tapped his pencil on the clipboard. "Of course you'll have to get a building permit from the city and another from the historical society."

He glanced toward her and kept his tone even. "Does this mean you're going to stay around for a while?"

"I don't know." She walked into the parlor and looked around. "Do you think I could take a few feet off this big room for a larger closet?"

He followed her. "Kate, does this mean you'll be staying in Silver Lake?" This time he spoke in a firm voice, a voice that expected an answer.

"I don't know." She turned toward him, biting her lip. "I really don't. I like my job. I dearly love Brooke. The town and the people and church—well, I feel at home here."

"That's because you *are* home."

"Yes, I know." She looked around as if searching for a place to avoid answering his question. "But Miami and Houston were my homes, too. I don't know if I want to go back there, but I don't know if I'd be happy here forever, either."

"Then why fix this place up?" He waved around the room.

"This is my house, too. I'm going to stay around for a few more months, even after Abby gets well. If I do leave, I'll have this apartment to come back to, something that's mine, not just a room in Abby's house."

He walked toward the proposed kitchen. "I can get an electrician here as soon as you get the permits if you decide to do this." He pointed at the wall. "He'll need to put an outlet for the stove here." He drew an X. "And some more up here for appliances."

"And a plumber?" she said from behind him.

"As soon as you get the permits." With a flip, he closed the clipboard. "Choose your cabinets and set up an appointment to have them put in. You could move in within a week or two after the paperwork's done."

Not much he could do about her uncertainty, but he could help her with this apartment. Whether that meant she stayed or left wasn't his call.

It never had been.

Six weeks after Abby's surgery, Kate studied catalogs of cabinets at the kitchen table. Because the renovations were minor, the building permit had been approved quickly and should arrive in a few days. The historical society indicated that as long as nothing on the outside was being disturbed and nothing was being changed in the older section of the house, the approval would come with no difficulty.

"What are you looking at, Aunt Kate?" Brooke entered the kitchen, shrugged off her backpack and placed it in the corner. Then she came around to look over Kate's shoulder. "You're looking at cabinets for your kitchen. Does that mean you're going to stay?"

"I'm considering it."

"Oh, I hope you do." Brooke put her arms around Kate's waist. "I really like to have you here."

Kate patted her niece's back. "I like being here." Then she glanced up.

Abby stood in the hall, leaning against the doorjamb and cradling her arm as she watched her daughter hug Kate. A look of shock and horror crossed her face before she turned and rushed away. Did she believe Kate had stolen her daughter?

Chapter Twelve

"What are you doing with Brooke?" Abby demanded when Kate checked on her a few hours later.

"I'm being her aunt." Kate placed a glass of tea on the table next to the place Abby did her exercises.

"I'm her mother," Abby said as she counted the number of repetitions for her arm lifts.

"Yes." No reason for arguments or fights. If she could just stay calm, Kate could handle this discussion, although staying calm in the demanding presence of her sister hadn't always been easy. It meant fighting the habit of, well, of her entire life in addition to Abby's ability to know exactly which of her sister's buttons to push for the most explosive reaction.

"Of course you're her mother, and I'm her aunt. Brooke is a lovely child. You should be proud to have a daughter like her."

Abby allowed the pulley to drop. "You know I am." A look of confusion covered her face, possibly because Kate hadn't lost her temper yet or because the compliment was so unexpected. With a glower, Abby asked, "Are you trying to take her away from me?"

Kate shook her head. "Abby, no one could take your daughter from you."

When Abby's expression didn't change but her gaze became sharper, Kate continued, "I'm not going to steal her from you. She loves me as an aunt, but she loves you as her mother."

"She never hugs me." Abby turned to hide her face and the pain Kate guessed was etched there.

"Maybe she doesn't know you'd like that." Kate wanted to ask if her sister ever hugged Brooke but decided not to. A little presumptuous for a childless woman to lecture her sister on child care. Abby would be sure to point that out.

"Of course she knows that." Abby's tone was sharp. "How could she not know that?"

"I don't know. You have to figure that out." Kate forced her mouth shut because she knew if she said anything more, the words would neither improve nor calm the relationship. She watched Abby stand and put her left hand on the back of the wooden chair and begin another set of exercises.

After a few minutes, she said, "Abby, there is something I want to apologize for." Kate took a deep breath. She might as well try this now because who knew when she'd get a better opportunity. "It has nothing to do with Brooke. I have to tell you I'm sorry about Joel, about how I flirted with him."

Abby lifted her gaze to study Kate. She shrugged, which brought a grimace of pain when she moved the sore shoulder. "Joel? I'd about forgotten about him."

Sure she had. The memory of that act was exactly why Abby thought Kate would steal her daughter.

"That was twenty years ago," Abby added.

"I know, and I never apologized. I was shallow and flirty—stupid." This confessing and asking for forgiveness was hard on the ego. With a deep breath, Kate said, "I'm sorry."

Abby finished her set, dropped her arm and walked across the floor to sit in an upholstered chair. "What I could never understand," she said. "What I could *never* understand is that everyone considered you a good Christian and yet you took my boyfriend and Sandra's." She shook her head. "How could you do that?"

"I was young and silly. Obviously my faith didn't shape my actions. I'm ashamed of that, truly." She settled on the footstool in front of her sister. "Please forgive me."

For a moment, Kate hoped her sister would say something or tell her to forget about the past; even making a gesture that showed she'd heard Kate's apology would be satisfactory.

Instead Abby leaned her head back. "I'm going to rest for a while."

Kate bit her lip as she watched Abby's features smooth out in relaxation. The lines of pain and just plain bad temper almost disappeared when she closed her eyes.

With a sigh, Kate stood. She'd tried and would keep trying. Abby was her only sister, and she wasn't about to give up on building that relationship.

But it would sure help if the other person involved were a little more cooperative.

Coco was limping badly. As Kate watched her pull herself up the ramp, her front legs scrabbled as she attempted to pull her rear legs behind her.

Kate had taken her to see Sara yesterday. Sara had given her a shot and some medicine, which she hoped might relieve the pain. She'd also said, "Kate, this dog is older than her years. She's a very stoic animal and is in a lot of pain."

Kate's sweet little Coco a stoic animal? She guessed she was.

But Sara's next words hit her like an escaped rottweiler.

"If the medication doesn't help, if she's still in pain, you're going to have to consider putting her to sleep."

Tears rolled down Kate's face as she lifted Coco. She held her pet in her arms and sobbed. Thank goodness she was alone. Abby would think she was nuts. Brooke would be heartbroken to know how poor Coco's health was. Lora would miss her puppy. And Rob...

And Rob had lost a wife. He'd probably think she was silly to care so much about a dog.

No, she knew that wasn't true. Rob had always loved animals. He'd know how she felt.

That evening, Rob came over with Lora and his mother to see the puppy. The three adults sat on the porch while Lora patted Coco, who lay quietly on the porch. Although the child called for Coco to join her in a romp across the lawn, Coco only lifted her head and smiled at Lora.

"What's wrong with Puppy?" Lora asked, her head tilted as she watched Coco snooze.

"She's getting old, Lora."

Lora walked to stand next to Kate's chair. "Getting old?"

"Her legs don't work as well as they used to and she wants to sleep a lot." Kate blinked to keep back tears, but Lora reached up and wiped them away with a tiny finger.

"Don't be sad, Miss Kate." She wiggled up on Kate's lap and put her arms around her to console her. The gesture felt so warm, so comforting that she held the little body close until, as expected, Lora wiggled off and skipped back to where Coco slept. As she patted the puppy several times, Coco licked her fingers.

When Coco fell asleep again and Lora began to yawn, Rob said to his mother, "Why don't you take her home and get her ready for bed."

Mrs. Chambers's glance moved from her son's face to Kate's.

"I'll be home soon, but I need to talk to Kate about that bedroom addition," he explained.

Mrs. Chambers smiled at Kate. "Thank you

for these nice evenings together. Lora and I both enjoy them." Then she took Lora's hand and allowed the child to lead her across the yard. At the gate, she turned around to look at the two and waved.

"Your daughter is darling," Kate said as she watched the child disappear inside the house.

"What can I say?" He grinned. "She's the joy of my life." He stood. "Let's look at the apartment again. I have an idea." He faced her. "At least if you're still planning to remodel it."

Beneath his words, she could hear an additional question, unspoken but clear nonetheless, asking if she was going to stay in Silver Lake.

"Yes." She led him toward the outside door. "I really like my job. Working for the newspaper is a lot of fun and I adore Mrs. Watkins, but it pays so little." She sighed and looked up at him just as they entered the rooms. "As much as I love it here, I may have to go someplace I can get a full-time job."

"You could commute. Austin isn't too far or you could work from home, on your computer."

"Possibly," she agreed.

He walked ahead of her to study the walls while she wondered what his suggestions about work meant. Was he being helpful in her job search or did he want her here, really want her to stay? Did she dare ask which?

Before she could make up her mind, he said, "I think if you pull this wall down between the parlor and the room you're going to use as the kitchen, it will make a nice open space." With his hands he showed her the divisions. "Kitchen, dining area, living area." He turned to look at her. "Do you still cook?"

"I mostly microwave stuff. None of the cakes and pies I made for the county fair."

"Too bad. They were great." He held out his laser measurer and placed it against the wall. "If you don't cook a lot, you don't need too big a kitchen. Maybe a galley type with a breakfast bar here?" He gestured toward a spot a few feet away.

"Perfect. A table there." She pointed. "And the rest as a living room." She turned around to study the suggested division of space. "I like that. I can watch television from the kitchen or chat with guests while I'm making dinner."

With the plans falling into place, except for that nagging worry about money, she felt happier than she had for a long time. This snug little place could be home, a place to entertain her friends and family. She could stay here and toss the baggage—both the boxes still in storage in Miami and the rough, emotional baggage from her previous life—she'd carried around with her for the past few years. Filled with delight, she smiled. "Oh, yes. I can see that."

She hadn't foreseen how that smile would affect Rob. He kept his eyes on her face but looked amazed, dazzled and pretty confused.

Then he took a step back.

Did that future include Rob? How could she know? The man still backed away from her.

"Guess that's it." Briskly he shoved the measuring device into his pocket and moved toward the door. Hastily.

The conference over, she walked behind Rob out to the porch. As usual, a breeze blew the scents of spring to them. Tonight the heavy scent of gardenias settled around them.

Soft music came from the Dkanys' house. Tonight Mrs. Dkany must have the remote because they were surrounded by the strains of a love song from the seventies.

Rob froze a moment when he heard the voice of Tony Bennett. She watched uncertainty play across his face when he stopped and looked down at her. As if he'd finally made up his mind, Rob took her hand. "Dance?"

With as much ease as she had years earlier, she stepped into his arms. Memories assaulted her: the prom, homecoming, casual evenings with their friends, all dancing on the porch. But as they swayed across the floor, she knew this was about more that the young Kate and Rob who used to dance to whatever music the Dkanys played. Tonight it was the older, experienced but perhaps still as foolish Kate and Rob who were in each other's arms, attempting to figure out who they were to each other.

Rob's body language spoke volumes. His rigid posture demonstrated he was not at all comfortable with the situation at the same time he held her firmly in his arms. The poor man was really conflicted.

Kate wasn't. She leaned her head on his chest, breathing in the smell of Rob: citrusy aftershave mixed with a little baby lotion. The scent wasn't at all romantic, but right now it seemed like it. His chest felt warm and hard against her cheek while his heart beat in counterpoint to the music.

Almost a minute passed before she realized the ballad had stopped and been replaced by a James Brown hit. Not exactly the perfect music for a romantic evening. Still she didn't pull away, too happy to be in exactly this place.

But Rob did. She glanced up at him when he again stepped away from her, dropping his arms to his sides. For a second, she saw wonder and happiness in his face but they were quickly replaced by the habitual smile that didn't really show much emotion. His eyes were unreadable again; his posture was tense and aloof.

"Good night," he said as if he hadn't been holding her in his arms only moments earlier.

She knew her face had shown how dazzled she'd been by his closeness, an expression quickly followed by surprise due to his cold response. "Good night." She stepped away from him. "Thank you for the consult."

He stepped off the porch. "Happy to do that for an old friend." With a two-fingered salute, he took off across the yard, loping as fast as possible, as if a terrible specter followed him. Perhaps it did. Perhaps he couldn't forget the memory of their own broken relationship or, more likely, the thought of Junie's death.

Whatever it was, his troubled expression told her if she really cared for Rob—as, she finally admitted to herself, she did—connecting with him, having him learn to trust her wasn't going to be easy. He'd built a mighty high wall around himself. Every now and then he allowed the defenses to fall, but it would take more than a kiss here and a dance and a canoe ride there to tear it down. Brick by brick was the only way she could see. She sighed. She was not a patient person and had no idea how to handle this, except with patience.

Settled in a chair, she could follow Rob's progress through the house as lights flicked on and off. In the kitchen, down the hall and upstairs, at last into what she guessed was Lora's room.

With that, she realized she was being too curious and nosy for her own good or Rob's. She closed her eyes and leaned back. Once comfortable, her worries settled over her like the clouds floating across the moon.

Listing her concerns, she knew Brooke was doing better and could cross her off the list. A job? She'd have to find a better one but her expenses weren't great. She could manage for a while, but, in the long run, she was going to have to make more money before her savings ran out.

And there was, of course, Abby.

What about her? Kate had read an article recently about depression. Could that be Abby's problem? Her sister had never been a happy person. Kate had considered herself the reason for Abby's grumpiness, but maybe that wasn't true. There could be physical problems, too.

How could she handle that? She most certainly couldn't say to Abby, "I think you may be clinically depressed." Well, she could and that was exactly what a loving sister would do, but those words would lead to denial, anger and unpleasantness from Abby. First, she should research depression, learn more about it before she did anything that would lead to further estrangement.

And Rob. What was she going to do about him? She didn't love him. Not yet, but that was the direction the relationship was heading, at least for her.

But not for him. Any feelings he had for her he sharply curtailed, pushing her away both physically and, more troubling, emotionally.

Trying to figure out what was going on with Rob was like a playing tug-of-war, but the line kept moving, first in one direction, then in the other. At one moment, they were getting close to each other. At another, it was as if she'd stepped into a pit of mud, alone.

Opening her eyes, she looked up at God's beautiful heavens. "Dear Lord, help me," she prayed. "I'm not the best person in the world.

I'm impatient and capricious, but I care about all these people very much." She stopped to consider what to say next then almost laughed at herself. God knew how she felt and who she was. She didn't need to censor her words. "Please help me know what to do, help me choose loving words and kind deeds. Help me follow where you lead." She pressed her hands more closely together. "And Rob." She took a deep breath and watched the clouds slip past the moon to bathe the world again in its light. "Please help me to know what to do about Rob."

"Aunt Kate, are you still out there?" Brooke shouted from the kitchen door. "I thought I heard you talking to someone."

"Just sitting here and looking at the sky."

"Do you mind if I interrupt you?" Her niece walked slowly toward her.

"You're not interrupting. Come sit down with me." Kate gestured toward the chair next to her.

"Thanks, but I've got homework tonight. I wondered if you could help me."

"What is it? Math is a puzzle to me, but I'm still pretty good in Spanish."

"It's a theme I have to write. Would you mind reading it?"

"Glad to." Kate pushed herself out of the chair. Before she followed Brooke into the house, she looked over her shoulder. There was a light on in the Chambers's house, downstairs. She wondered if Rob was thinking about her as she was of him.

After work two days later, Kate parked in front of the house.

Almost seven weeks after surgery, Abby was doing much better, moving around on her own, but still couldn't drive, not with the large immobilizer that kept her arm in place.

After taking a bundle of letters from the mailbox, Kate flipped through them and found an official-looking document from the historical society. She tore the envelope open as she headed toward the house and scanned it. Her permit. Since the city had approved her building permit, she could begin construction on the apartment. She'd call Rob this afternoon and ask him about the electrician.

Once inside, she carefully placed the rest of the mail in the basket on the front table and headed toward the kitchen for a glass of tea. As she approached the door, she heard soft snuffling sounds, like sobs.

Inside, Brooke sat at the table, her head in her

arms and crying. Kate immediately dropped into a chair next to her and began rubbing her back.

"What is it, sweetheart? Are you okay?"

Brooke kept weeping until finally she whispered, "Marta Elisa."

"Marta Elisa?" Kate pulled a tissue from her purse. "Is Marta Elisa hurt?"

"No, she's fine." Brooke dabbed her eyes with the tissue but that didn't stop the flow of tears down her cheeks. "She's getting adopted."

Kate started to say, "How wonderful," but changed her words when she saw the misery in Brooke's eyes. "You're going to miss her."

"She's leaving in four weeks, after school's out." Brooke's lower lip trembled. "Am I the worst friend in the world not to want her to go?"

"Of course you're not." Kate put her arm around her niece's shoulder. "She's your friend. You're glad deep inside that she's going to have a family, but you'll miss her."

When she heard a slight sound in the hall, Kate glanced up. Abby stood there in black slacks and the white Oxford cloth shirt Kate had helped her put on that morning. Abby's glare showed her thoughts so clearly.

No, Kate wasn't stealing her daughter, but Abby had to start acting like a mother or Brooke would start turning more and more to Kate. After a glare at her sister, Kate turned back to Brooke. "Why don't you tell your mother about this?"

The alien-visitor expression momentarily wiped the grief from Brooke's face. Kate nudged her.

"Marta Elisa is getting adopted and moving to San Antonio," Brooke told her mother.

Abby started to shrug but Kate's furious glower stopped her. "Why don't you tell your mother about it," Kate repeated slowly, giving special emphasis to her words. Would Abby understand what she meant?

Kate stood, pulled her niece up with her and gave her a hard shove toward her mother. Just as she did, amazingly Abby reached the one good arm toward her daughter.

Brooke looked first at her mother, followed by a glance at Kate, who gave her another push, then Brooke ran to Abby. "I'm going to really miss her," she said as she threw herself against her mother's chest.

Abby held her daughter as if she were a bundle of brittle sticks. Nonetheless, she comforted her with awkward little pats to Brooke's shoulder. Seeing Abby make an effort to be maternal, Kate slipped out to the back porch and sat down, rubbing Coco's ears. And she smiled.

"Thank you, Lord, for your guidance."

Chapter Thirteen

There were times life confounded Rob.

In his rational world, one thing followed another. Reasonably. In a blueprint, there were set regulations about electrical usage and metal stress. Everything followed a set of sound guidelines.

Architecture used straight lines and right angles. It was clean, clear and concise, only occasionally cluttered with arcs and circles.

He should have learned years ago that life didn't follow rules or reason. No matter how hard he'd tried to force life into grids and charts, it was messy. It spilled over, outside the lines. Life was nothing like the logical beauty of architecture.

His relationship with Kate was the messiest, most unpredictable, most illogical part of his world at this moment. Probably ever. He didn't trust his feelings about Kate so he kept pulling away. He knew she would send his rational, reasonable life into a tailspin if he allowed that. He did not need, want, hope for or seek another tailspin.

For two days, he'd kept his distance after the dance that had forced him to reexamine who he was and what he wanted in life. However, whenever he saw her, logic and reason no longer mattered to him.

He was a mature man, a widower with a young daughter and an exhausting business, a man with clearly defined responsibilities. That was who he was. He was not the sort of man who mooned around about an old girl-friend. He *knew* with deep certainty and every iota of his being that Kate would mess up his nice, logical plans, but when he held her in his arms, certainty and logic no longer mattered to him.

So forty-eight hours earlier, he'd run. Turned away and headed home.

Not that what he did made sense. It didn't even make him happy and wasn't fair to Kate. Several times a day, he looked out the window to try to catch a glimpse of her. If he didn't see her, he felt disappointed. If he did, he felt stupid because why was he hiding in here when all he wanted was to be with Kate?

Simple. He was acting like a scared kid. He'd thought he'd reached a place in life where he made good, mature, intelligent decisions.

What now?

Maybe he should pray. That's what he'd done almost constantly when Junie got sick. That's what his mother still told him to do. He believed in prayer, even knelt beside Lora every night as she prayed before he tucked her in bed.

But, after Junie died, he didn't *trust* prayer. Even worse, he was beginning to realize he didn't trust God, either.

Which left him pretty much alone in the middle of his logical, linear world.

The realization of his self-imposed isolation made him stand and stare out the window. Of course his eyes leaped immediately to where Kate sat on the porch with her dog. The longer he watched her, the more he didn't care if she fit in his life exactly. He wanted to see if by moving some lines and opening some space, there would be room for her. And him. Together.

Even if she left, he had to try. He had to know. He had to behave like an adult and work the situation out like a mature man. He turned off the light and ambled outside and through the alley.

"Want some company?" Talk about a stupid line, but it was the best he'd come up with on the walk over.

She nodded. "Please."

From Goliad Street in front of the Wallaces' house, he could hear the engines of a few cars, people heading home from work to be with family. From the Dkaneys' came the sound of Winona.

A breeze ruffled the apple trees, surrounding them with a light, sweet scent. It also tousled Kate's hair, which had grown a little since she'd arrived, making her look younger and not quite so, well, professional. Odd he'd seen that. Junie had always said he was the most unobservant man in the world, that she could shave her head and he wouldn't notice.

But he didn't want to think about Junie now.

"Do you want to get some dinner? Mom took Lora to visit Aunt Pris in Lampasas and I'm on my own."

"Sure." She stood. "Do I need to change clothes?"

She wore a black Silver Lake High School T-shirt with jeans and sandals. "You look fine for Storms."

"Great." She grinned. "I haven't been there since I got back. I've missed their onion rings."

"Come on. We can take my truck." He started toward his yard.

"Let me tell Abby where I'm going."

He watched her lean her head inside the house, talk for a minute, then reach down and pat Coco before she started toward him.

"Do you want to bring the dog? We can go through the drive-in."

"No." She shook her head. "She's tired now." She reached the truck and pulled herself into the seat. "I took her to see Sara again yesterday. She says Coco's not responding to the arthritis medication so she's trying something else, but that Coco's an old dog." Her fists clenched in her lap.

Rob hated to see the sadness in Kate's expression so he started the truck, headed down the driveway and changed the subject. "How's the remodeling on the house coming?"

"Great. I talked to…"

An hour later, he parked the pickup in his driveway. His mother's parking space stood empty so she didn't need to know about tonight's impromptu date.

What? He didn't want his mother to know that he'd taken Kate to Storms? Besides, this wasn't a date and, even if it were, why would he need to hide it from his mother? He was thirty-four years old and wasn't going to hurry Kate home so his mother wouldn't find out where he'd been. He cut off the engine and glanced at Kate.

"Thanks for dinner." She shoved a couple of crumpled napkins in the litter bag. "That meal was filling and nutritious, and probably contained enough cholesterol to clog my arteries for the rest of my life."

"You probably didn't get enough in Miami. Needed to come home to get real food." He swung from the cab, closed his door and walked to her side of the truck.

"Lard, Rob, lard. That's what they cook with in Miami. And cheese." She placed her hand on the arm he held out. "It's not as bad as chicken fried steak with thick white gravy and chili cheese fries in Texas, but I've yet to live anyplace that didn't have food that could put ten pounds on you just by walking close to it."

As he walked her across the alley to her house, Rob enjoyed the feeling of her next to him, the warmth of her hand on his arm and, well, just the closeness of Kate.

Dusk was falling but it wasn't dark yet. Not dark enough to steal a kiss because he knew the neighbors would be watching. Mr. and Mrs. Norton were gardening. Country music still came from the Dkany home and he figured Trixie and Paul were sitting on the back porch, as usual.

"Do you want to come in and see Abby?"

He couldn't refuse, so he followed Kate inside, spent a few minutes chatting with Abby in the parlor, then half an hour enjoying a slice of apple pie before he decided he'd better go home.

By the time Kate walked him out on the back porch, his mother had returned home, her blue Volvo pulled up next to her apartment.

"I like the geraniums." He watched the hummingbirds drinking from the flowers and stalled for a few more minutes with her. "What happened to your plan for a garden?"

"Don't ask. Abby's already scolded me about that."

He scowled. "She scolded you about the garden?"

"Not that, really, only the fact that I don't finish what I start."

"What?"

"Well, I left you, number one." She counted on her fingers. "I left my family, that's second. My sister and I don't get along. I didn't even know my niece or when she was born. I had to leave my job. There's even the garden I never planted." She shrugged. "I don't finish what I start. I have no stick-to-itiveness."

"Kate, Kate, Kate." He leaned his head back and laughed.

"What?" Her voice sounded a little insulted.

"You don't have any idea what an amazing woman you are, do you?"

"Oh?" She tilted her head in interest.

"The reason you didn't finish a few things is that your dreams are so much bigger than anyone else's. You shot high."

"What do you mean?"

He gazed down at her. "You left Silver Lake because your dreams were so huge our little town couldn't hold them. You worked hard and got better and better positions. Probably would have been a senator someday if your crooked boss hadn't let you down."

"I was shooting for White House spokes-person."

He laughed. "You come home and after a few weeks, you brought your sister and Brooke together. I don't know if you and Abby will ever be close, but not because you aren't trying."

"She's my sister, Rob. I have to do something."

"Kate, you can't fix her. You can't *make* her be happy."

"Oh." She considered that for a moment. "I'd never thought of it that way. I didn't realize I was trying to fix her." She laughed. "I guess that's what I do."

"As for the garden, I watched you work on it."

"You did?"

"You dug for hours. You worked as hard as any of my construction people."

"But I didn't finish."

He laughed and hugged her. "Kate, that garden took years to grow. Your mother constantly worked on it, experimented with new plants, expanded it every year. Only you would believe you could do that by sheer force of will in a few days." He shook his head. "You've always been impatient and demanded a lot of yourself because your dreams are so big."

"You really believe that?"

"I really believe that." He put his hand on her cheek and rubbed softly with his thumb. "You've always been determined to fix every single problem in the world. You can't but you always try. I admire that."

She gazed at him through the dark and he

realized how close they had become. He did admire her but his feelings had expanded far past that. He put his hand on her cheek for a second before he said, "I'd better go."

"I'll get the yard light for you."

But when she stood and reached out to flip the porch light on, he put his hand over hers. She glanced at him in surprise, then smiled when she saw him lean toward her.

He took her into his arms and lowered his lips to hers. In the darkness, he could feel as if they were alone, as if only the two of them existed with no problems and no past to separate them.

Then logic returned. How, exactly, even a sliver of sense penetrated the pleasure of Kate's kiss, he didn't know. He *did* know the exact reason he was glad it was dark and no one could see them. It was better for both of them not to broadcast the news that Rob Chambers was falling in love with Kate Wallace. Again.

The next afternoon, Kate stood in the middle of the partially completed kitchen and grinned. Yes, the remodel had taken several thousand dollars from savings, but it was worth it. She had a place of her own.

The electricity was hooked up. A hole in the countertop showed where the sink would be. Another marked where the cooktop would be dropped. Used appliances added to furniture from the storeroom would fill in the other places.

"Looks good," Abby observed from the parlor.

"Thanks. Do you want to see the rest? I painted the bedroom this morning."

Abby didn't move from the wall. Instead she wrinkled her nose. "I know. I could smell it."

Kate sighed. Didn't look as if they'd ever be close sisters, but at least they were talking more. Well, talking a little. An improvement.

"So?" Abby watched her sister but gave away no emotion. "Are you staying?"

"I think so."

"Does that depend on Rob? Does he want you to stay?"

"No, and I don't know." Kate shook her head. "The decision depends on if I can find a job here. Rob and I haven't discussed the future." Kate took a step toward her sister. "After all, I've only been home seven weeks."

"You're adults. That's enough time to know." Abby paused while she gave the room a once-over. "Except he's still in love with his wife." She disappeared back into the parlor.

Yes, she'd been here seven weeks. Abby would go back to work in a few days although Kate would drive her around for another week.

Then what?

And how could she find out if what Abby said was true and Rob was still in love with his wife?

When Kate got home from work Tuesday, she went to the backyard and called, "Coco." The cocker didn't bark or trot over to greet her.

Poor old creature. She was probably dozing in the shade. The dog was doing more sleeping than ever and her climb up the ramp became slower every day. Kate needed to make a decision about her, but she wasn't ready. Not yet. She needed Coco around for the next part of their lives. Maybe once their future was decided and sure...

"Coco?" she called, then saw the little dog lying in the shade of the apple tree, a few blossoms covering her side.

Filled with dread, Kate ran to Coco, tossed her purse aside and kneeled next to the cocker, putting her hand on the dog's side. Although the cocker's breathing was shallow, her lungs rose and fell under Kate's hand. That was a good sign, wasn't it?

"Coco?" she whispered. Coco opened her eyes and smiled a bit. When Kate put her hand under the dog's chin, Coco licked it, then closed her eyes.

Tears began to flow down Kate's cheeks. "Coco? Oh, please, no."

One thought filled Kate's head: get Coco to the veterinarian. She slid her arms under the animal and lifted gently, but a moan broke through the dog's lips and her eyelids fluttered. When Kate realized she was hurting the cocker, she laid her back on the grass and put her hand on Coco's side to feel the shallow respiration.

With tears obscuring her vision, Kate grabbed her purse, fumbled for the phone and hit speed dial for Sara's office.

"This is Kate Wallace," she said to the receptionist. "I need to talk to Sara, please." When the veterinarian came on the line, Kate explained what had happened. "I can't bring her in. She's in too much pain."

"I'll be right there."

"Aunt Kate, what happened?" Brooke stood on the porch, still wearing her backpack from school, and watched as her aunt sobbed and patted the cocker. "Is Coco sick?"

"I'm afraid so." Kate forced the words out.

"Oh, no." Brooke shrugged the backpack off and threw it on a chair before she jumped off the porch and ran to where Kate kneeled. She settled next to her aunt, placed her hand on Coco's head and scratched.

"Sara's coming over now." Kate kept one hand on her pet and used the other to wipe tears away.

"Maybe she's just really sleepy. Or maybe she needs a drink of water." But Brooke's wavering voice said she didn't believe that.

Only a few minutes later, they heard a car pull up in the driveway and footsteps running up the driveway and through the gate. Kate moved out of the way when Sara placed a small black bag next to the dog and pulled out a stethoscope. She placed it against Coco's chest and listened. In only seconds, Sara sat back on her heels and shook her head.

"She's very weak, Kate. She's an old dog with severe health problems." Sara placed her hand on top of Kate's. "She's in a lot of pain and the medication isn't working. She isn't going to get better. You have to make this decision for her."

"I can't," Kate whispered. But she was the only one who could. She swallowed hard and attempted to form the words but they choked her before she could say anything. Finally she said in a voice so thin and wavering she didn't recognize it as her own, "Do what's best." She drew a deep breath. "Put her to sleep."

Sara opened the case again and took out several alcohol swabs. She cleaned an area on Coco's leg then pulled a syringe from the bag. After filling it from a vial, she glanced at Kate and Brooke. "Say goodbye," she said softly.

Kate scratched Coco's head. "Goodbye, little friend."

Brooke rubbed her hand down the dog's back and sobbed.

After Sara finished the injection, she placed the stethoscope on Coco's chest. Within a few seconds, she said, "She's gone." She placed her hand on Coco's head and smoothed the fur back. "She was a sweet old girl. She's out of pain now, Kate."

The three kneeled there for a minute before Sara asked, "What do you want to do with her? We can bury her behind the clinic."

"No." Brooke straightened and wiped the tears with the back of her hand. "We need to bury her back here. Under her tree."

Sara put her instruments back in the bag, closed it and stood. "I'm sorry to rush off. I have to get back to the office. I'll call later."

Kate stood next to her and took her friend's hand. "Thanks for coming."

With a hug, Sara spun and headed back across the yard.

"I'll get the shovels, Aunt Kate." Brooke moved toward the shed, opened the door and disappeared for a moment. She came back with two shovels and handed one to Kate. "How 'bout right here?" She pointed to where Coco lay. "That was her favorite place."

With a nod, Kate gently lifted the dog's warm body out of the way.

It took a long time for the two of them to make a dent in the ground. After fifteen minutes, they'd dug through the grass and a couple more inches of dirt, but the ground was clay, hard and dry with a few rocks mixed in to dull the shovels and make the task more difficult.

Fifteen minutes later, they'd dug down a few more inches and had removed a dozen rocks, but the hole wasn't nearly wide enough or deep enough for the small body. Leaning on the shovels, they took a few minutes to rest.

"I'll ask Rob if he can help," Brooke said.

Kate hated to interrupt Rob at work, but she didn't see any choice. She and Brooke could dig for hours and still not have a hole large enough.

Within a few minutes, Rob crossed the alley. "Brooke says Coco died."

Kate tried to keep her chin from wavering and brushed back tears with a tissue. Of course Rob could see her red eyes. He'd know how upset she was. "Yes, she just wore out."

"You're going to miss her."

She nodded but couldn't say anything.

Without a word, Rob picked up a shovel and began to dig.

Within twenty minutes, he had a nice-size hole dug. After fifteen more, it was deep enough.

While he worked, Brooke ran inside and came back with a soft blue blanket. With great care, Kate lifted Coco onto the blanket and Brooke wrapped her up.

"Okay, ladies." Rob leaned the shovel against a tree as perspiration ran down his face and stained his knit shirt. "This should be the right size."

Brooke placed Coco in the hole and she and Kate shoveled dirt and rocks into the opening, tamping it down then leaving a slight mound above it. When they stood back, Kate folded Brooke in her arms as they both cried.

"I have to go tell my mother." Brooke patted her aunt on the shoulder. "I have to go tell Mom," Brooke repeated.

Kate watched her niece head toward the house.

"Don't you think you're making too much of this?" Rob asked in a harsh but quiet voice.

Shocked, Kate swung around to look at him. His jaw was clenched, a muscle twitching along the right side.

"Kate, I know you cared about Coco, but you have to be strong." He nodded toward the porch. "Look at Brooke and how upset she is."

She glanced toward the house but Brooke was already inside. "She cared about Coco, too."

"But she's a child. You're an adult. You have to be strong so she won't feel so bad."

"Rob, no matter what I do, Brooke's going to feel terrible. She loved Coco."

"Kate, you're making it worse. Don't you see?"

She couldn't believe she and Rob were having this conversation such a short time after they'd buried Coco. She shook her head. "I think crying when someone dies is normal."

"When Junie died, I kept strong, Kate. No one saw me cry. I set an example."

"Why?" She lifted her eyes to his face, which was stony cold. "Why? You'd just lost your wife. People would expect you to grieve."

"I had a daughter, a baby daughter, a business to run, lots of responsibilities." He nodded toward the house. "Look how unhappy Brooke is. If you were stronger, she wouldn't hurt so much."

Kate blinked and attempted to take in Rob's words. "But when you love someone, even if it's a silly little cocker spaniel, it's going to hurt when they're gone. Mourning that death means the creature was important to you."

"But it doesn't solve anything. It won't bring her back."

"Well, of course not." She continued to study Rob. Was he talking about Coco or Junie? He refused to meet her eyes, keeping his gaze over her head. How could she reach him when he'd cut himself off?

Then as she watched, a thought struck her and, unthinking, she voiced it. "Rob, have you grieved for the loss of Junie?"

As soon as she blurted the words, Kate recognized her terrible mistake. What an awful, thoughtless question to ask a man who'd lost his wife.

"That's none of your business," he said, his voice cold and clear. "We're not talking about me." He bit off each word.

"I'm sorry. I had no right…"

But he didn't listen to her apology. He turned away from her and stalked toward the alley, slamming the gate behind him with a crack that echoed through the yard.

"Aunt Kate," Brooke called from the kitchen door. "Do you want some lemonade? A glass of water?"

She nodded and headed into the house walking mechanically and feeling so cold. Coco had died and Rob... She'd hurt Rob deeply.

As she walked, she remembered her words and Rob's swift reaction. How could she have been so thoughtless? She'd hurt him deeply and she hated that.

After what she'd said, it would be a long time before she saw Rob Chambers again. And she didn't blame him a bit.

Chapter Fourteen

Her big mouth had gotten Kate in trouble again. Why hadn't she learned to keep it closed? The pushy woman who lived inside her escaped way too often. Although that quality had served her well as a reporter and a press secretary, she'd never learned to handle real people, people outside politics, normal people, nearly as well.

But this was more than being in trouble. She'd hurt Rob, deeply. She'd judged his feelings for his wife and his reaction to her death.

How could she have done that? How? And why? The answers she came up with made her cringe. She was insensitive and hypercritical and probably, if she were honest, possessed a lot more negative traits than she wanted to list at the moment.

That evening, she watched the Chambers's house from the French door to her apartment. No lights were on that she could see, only a glow coming from Mrs. Chambers's apartment.

"Aunt Kate?" Brooke knocked on the door from the parlor and entered after Kate said, "Come in."

In her hand, Brooke held a plate with a huge slice of chocolate cake, the last piece of another red velvet cake Miss Betsy had sent over a few days earlier. "Here," Brooke said.

"Thank you." Kate smiled. "You take it." But, at Brooke's disappointed expression, Kate said, "Let's share it. Get another fork from my kitchen."

As they settled down to eat, Brooke asked, "How are you doing?"

"I miss Coco. Tonight will be the first time in a long time she hasn't slept at my feet."

"She was in pain. It was better for her." Brooke patted her aunt's shoulder but tears sparkled in her eyes.

"Yes, it was, but sometimes what's better for others doesn't feel best for us."

After she took the last bit of cake and slid her fork around the plate to get every smidgen of frosting, Brooke said, "Aunt Kate, please don't leave Silver Lake. I'd miss you."

"If I could find a job, I'd stay around. I like it here." She hugged Brooke. "I like being with my family."

"Maybe you could write a book and get rich and famous. Then you could stay."

Kate laughed, a sad little sound because she still missed having Coco's head on her foot but a laugh nonetheless. "Yes, writing a bestseller and making a lot of money would help a lot, but that seldom happens."

"You could get another job."

"I'm looking."

She'd have to sit down with a pencil and decide how much money she'd need to afford to live here. Of course she should have done that before, when she first considered staying, but with her usual headstrong rush, she hadn't.

Brooke stood. "I saw you talking to Rob after I came inside. He looked angry."

Kate nodded. "I said something I shouldn't have."

"Shouldn't you apologize?"

"Yes, I did but…" She shrugged because she didn't want to explain further. "Do you want to come out on the porch with me?"

"Thanks, Aunt Kate, but I have a spelling test tomorrow. Mom's going to quiz me over the words."

When her niece left, Kate wandered out on the porch alone and settled in the chair. She missed having Coco hobbling along behind her, settling next to her on the floor and putting her head up for Kate to scratch. She fought tears, without complete success.

But mourning Coco wasn't why she'd come out here. She wanted time to meditate, decide what she had to do to repair the damage she'd caused. Even if there could never be anything between her and Rob, she needed to, had to, apologize to him again for her careless words.

Before she could form a plan, she heard Lora's laugh from the alley and, almost immediately, the sound of Mrs. Chambers calling, "Lora, come back."

Within a few seconds, Lora burst through the gate and shouted, "Puppy." Because the child had such a big smile, Kate knew Lora didn't know Coco had died. She also knew Rob would be really furious if she told his daughter about Coco's death.

Lora trotted across the yard, stood in front of Kate with her hands on her hips and her curls bouncing. "Where's Puppy?"

Kate stood, walked down the steps and kneeled to be Lora's height. "Lora, didn't I tell you that you cannot see Coco unless your father or your grandmother calls first?"

"No, I…" But the child stopped her words and nodded.

Mrs. Chambers rushed through the gate and stopped when she saw Lora and Kate deep in conversation.

"Nobody called me, Lora. Neither your father nor your grandmother called to ask if you could come over to see the puppy."

"Nobody called." Lora shook her head, putting so much pitiful dejection in her words and expression that Kate might have relented if it had been possible to bring Coco to see Lora.

"You can't see Coco tonight." Kate stood. "You have to remember the rules. You can't run away from your grandmother."

"You must ask permission," Mrs. Chambers added. Then she whispered, "Thank you," at exactly the same time they heard someone else run down the alley and burst into the backyard.

Rob stood at the gate breathing hard, an expression of worry marking his face.

Lora turned toward her father, her expression showing she knew she was in big trouble. "I want to see Puppy," she explained sweetly.

"I told Lora she couldn't see the puppy

tonight because she didn't ask permission," Kate explained.

Rob relaxed. "Thank you." Then he said to his mother, "Why don't you take Lora home. I need to talk to Kate a minute."

As the two disappeared, he said, "Thank you for not telling her."

"Sooner or later, someone's going to have to tell Lora the puppy is dead. Or that she's on a long trip. Your daughter's smart. She's going to notice Coco's not here and you can't lie to her."

"I know."

Kate didn't believe his jaw could have become more determined, but it did.

"I'll take care of that in a way that won't upset her," he said. "In my way and time."

"She should be upset."

"Kate, she's barely three."

"But…" Kate stopped. If she knew anything it was that she didn't have the experience or the right to tell a father how to raise his daughter. She closed her mouth firmly and nodded.

"*I'll* tell her." He gestured toward himself with his thumb.

Having made sure that Kate knew she wasn't to say a word, he stepped back and headed toward his yard.

As she looked at his straight, rigid back, his shoulders firm and resolute, Kate knew she had to say something even though she was pretty sure he wasn't going to listen.

"Rob, I'm sorry. I shouldn't have said what I did. Not just about Lora and Coco. I shouldn't have said anything about how you handled Junie's death."

He didn't turn around. He didn't slow his pace.

"I'm really sorry." She took a step toward him and held out her hands but he kept going, didn't look back.

When he left the yard, the sound of an old Beatles song floated across from the Dkanys' house. She wondered if he'd ever be back, if they'd ever dance together again under the silver moonlight, if they'd even know each other when they were sixty-four.

Thursday afternoon, Mrs. Watkins called Kate to her office. "I have a proposition for you." The editor removed her reading glasses with huge, pink frames and tapped them on the desk. "Arnold's upset because he thinks I spend too much time at the paper."

"Oh? I'm sorry." Was that the correct response? Kate didn't know.

"He said he bought me the paper to keep me busy after I retired, but I'm spending more time working here than with him." She shoved her drooping mound of big Texas hair a little to the right. "Now that he's retired, Arnold wants to travel."

Kate nodded. Made sense. But what did it mean to her? she wondered selfishly.

"So my choice is my husband or the paper and, despite all I may have said about Arnold, I'd miss him." She nodded and her hair shook a little. "So, I have a proposition for you, one I'd never make to anyone else."

For a few seconds, Mrs. Watkins didn't say a word, just continued to stare at her ring. The lengthening silence worried Kate. Finally Mrs. Watkins lifted her gaze and said, "I want to hire you to run the paper."

Kate leaned back in her chair, partially in shock, partially in relief. "You want me to run the paper? The *Sentinel?*"

Mrs. Watkins nodded. "If you weren't around, we'd probably have to sell, but Arnold likes the investment and I'm fond of the place. I wouldn't give up working here completely, but you'd be the boss. You'd be completely in charge."

Kate couldn't form an answer.

"You probably wonder how much we'd pay you." She mentioned a figure.

Pulling her thoughts together, Kate sat forward. "I'm very interested, but I'll have to think it over. I need to figure out if I can afford to do this and if it's what I really want to do." She shook her head. "I'm still in shock. I'd never considered running the paper to be a possibility."

But she was pretty sure she'd accept. The increased salary balanced things out very well for her. She could even put money back into her savings.

Mrs. Watkins nodded. "Think about it, okay?"

The previous evening, the Dkanys' visiting grandsons had moved furniture into the apartment: her bed, the card table and four folding chairs for the dining area, a floor lamp, and, in front of the television, a comfortable blue plaid chair with matching ottoman. She'd hung blue curtains that afternoon as well as a few pictures from the storeroom. The painting over the sofa was a spring scene, which showed brilliant bluebonnets mixed with a scattering of Indian blankets along a dusty, winding road.

For a moment she looked at the apartment.

Warm, comfortable and hers. She settled at the table with a calculator and paper and jotted some numbers down.

That finished, she put down the pencil, closed her eyes and folded her hands. "Dear Lord," she prayed. "I have a decision to make, and I need to make it with you. Please, loving God, please help me to do your will, to be your person, to find my place to serve. Please guide me to use the talents you gave me to glorify you."

For a few more minutes she sat, her head bowed, and listened.

When she opened her eyes again, she'd made up her mind. Even if Rob wasn't part of her future, Silver Lake was home. She wanted to watch Brooke grow up, attend church and witness, stay with Sara and watch her friend's children grow up. And try to become closer to her sister.

If Rob didn't fit into her future, Silver Lake did.

"Thank you, Lord, for bringing me home."

Three days later, she and Brooke again walked to church. She greeted Mrs. Oglesby and the other friendly members, then joined Sara in her pew. Brooke sat next to Marta Elisa and on the other side of a new foster child.

Before the service began, Kate glanced up from the bulletin to see Sandra Dolinski walking down the aisle with two young children, then pause to speak to Mrs. Oglesby.

"I need to apologize to Sandra someday," Kate whispered to Sara.

"Why?"

"Well, because I took her boyfriend."

"That was almost twenty years ago."

"Yes, but I still…"

Sara glanced from Kate to Sandra. "She should thank you. That guy was a creep. She married a wonderful man and has two darling children. And her name is Sandra Martinez now."

"But I…"

Sara began to rise to her feet. "I'll tell her that. I'll tell her to stop giving you a rough time because she owes you an apology for being rude to you."

"No." Kate grabbed her arm and pulled her down on the pew. "Don't do that."

"If you really feel you have to apologize, do that sometime, but don't stew about it."

Kate smiled to herself. Another example of trying to fix things. Both she and Sara had problems with that.

When the service began, she noticed that

Rob sat on the other side of the congregation with his mother and Lora. After the children's moment, Lora followed the other children out of the sanctuary, waving at Kate as she left.

But Rob didn't notice her or had tried not to. After the service, Mrs. Chambers greeted her, but Rob had hurried out to find Lora in the nursery.

That afternoon, Kate pulled the porch table by her chair and spread out newspapers from other small towns. With a highlighter, she circled ideas she liked or crossed out what she didn't. As she jotted down a few notes, she again heard Lora in the alley, but the child walked slowly and wasn't smiling when she entered the gate. Mrs. Chambers entered the yard behind her.

"Where's Puppy?" Lora glanced at the mound under the tree.

"It's all right, Kate. Rob told her." Mrs. Chambers patted her granddaughter on the shoulder. "She wants to see where you buried her."

Kate stood and walked toward the child, then kneeled next to her. "You know that Coco died?"

Lora nodded, tears springing to her eyes. "Coco's gone."

"Yes, her legs hurt."

Lora shook her head. "Didn't want to play."

"No, she didn't. She was tired, but she was a sweet old dog, wasn't she?"

The child nodded.

"Brooke and I buried her right there, under the tree." Lora pointed. "Your father dug the hole."

Solemnly Lora walked to the place and put her hand on the top of the mound of dirt. After a short pause, Lora said, "My mommy died."

"Yes, sweetheart. I know that."

"She's in heaven."

Kate nodded.

"Is Coco with my mommy in heaven?"

Kate almost gasped. She was in no way prepared to discuss the theological issues of whether or not pets went to heaven with a child. What could she say?

"She'll be where all loving pets go," said Mrs. Chambers, who obviously had a great deal more experience answering children's questions than Kate.

The explanation satisfied Lora.

"Thank you for letting me bring her over," Mrs. Chambers said. "No matter what Rob says, she needed to say goodbye to Coco."

Kate raised an eyebrow, uncertain how to answer that.

"I know he's angry with you about something, but I thank you, Kate. He's been in a state of grief and denial for two years. He needed to be shaken up."

"But, Mrs. Chambers, I was so rude. I feel terrible."

"You must have said what he needed to hear." Mrs. Chambers put her hand on Kate's shoulder. "Thank you. And, please, call me Patricia."

Spring was speeding past. Kate had arrived in late March, just as the bluebonnets were blooming. They'd long since disappeared. April was gone, May was half over. The cactus flowers lingered as did the pink evening primrose.

School would be out in two weeks, and, as Brooke had mentioned at least five times a day, Marta Elisa would be moving but the girls had plans to visit each other.

In only an hour on this warm Sunday afternoon, the backyard would be filled with Marta Elisa's friends and family, including her new family, anxious to take her home the day summer vacation started. All her friends in Silver Lake were coming tonight to tell her goodbye and how much they loved her.

In the past week, Kate had taken over for Mrs. Watkins, moving into her office and making a few changes. Abby's sling had come off a week earlier, new exercises had been added to her physical therapy and she had almost complete use of the arm. That meant Kate no longer had to work around her sister's schedule.

Lora and Mrs. Chambers—Patricia—came over once or twice a week for cookies. Brooke had signed up for swimming lessons and was making plans to visit her father in August. The mound beneath which Coco lay had shrunk with the spring rain and Kate had nearly become used to the absence of her cocker. Life went on.

And yet, nothing had changed between her and Rob.

Kate was determined not to toss Rob away as she had before. By watching over Lora, by attending church, by being a good neighbor, she'd tried to convince him she'd be with him as he struggled. All this in the hope she could teach Rob to trust her, so he could believe she wasn't going to leave him as she had before, as Junie had with her death.

But it didn't look as if anything she did made the slightest difference. Rob only nodded to her at church. A slight improvement but she feared only because he was too polite to ignore her.

"Aunt Kate, where do you want the napkins and plates?"

Kate awakened from her reverie and smiled at her niece. "I think we'll serve everything from the kitchen counter, then come out here to eat. We'll grill the hamburgers and hot dogs out there." She pointed to the grill by the porch. "Sara can serve them when people have their plates ready. Does that sound okay?"

Brooke nodded. "Sounds good. Anything else we need to do?"

"I can't think of anything more to do until the guests start arriving."

When Brooke left, Kate settled into one of the chairs and leaned back against the new cushions she and Abby had bought. Her thoughts turned back to Rob.

Practicing patience and prayer, she hoped she and Rob could work things out, that they could find each other, that they could build a life together. She didn't know what more she could do. "Dear Lord, it's in your hands now."

Lora held one of Rob's hands as they walked through the alley. In the other, she held a gift bag covered with yellow flowers, a present for Marta, who had been so sweet to Lora at church, often helping in the nursery.

He'd asked his mother to take Lora to the party, but she'd refused. Something about her lumbago, she'd said.

His mother no more had lumbago than he had whooping cough, but the determination in her voice told him she'd made up her mind. He'd have to take his daughter to the farewell party.

So here he was. The thought of being close to Kate filled him with dread. There was so much he didn't understand about himself and his feelings, which was really stupid for a thirty-four-year-old man. Why was he such a jerk?

As he and Lora left the house, his mother had said, "Stop hiding. Kate's not a man-eating tiger."

He thought he could face a tiger with more courage than he could summon up to spend a few hours in the backyard of the pretty blonde who waited to serve him cake and ice cream.

The place was crowded. Probably twenty-five kids of all ages and nearly the same number of adults. Eating at tables on the porch, going in and out of the house with plates of food, running across the lawn playing tag, settling on blankets by the fence and enjoying dinner. The Dkaneys supplied soft music, country, oldies and a few new songs from the White Stripes.

While Sara stood at the grill, Kate and Brooke wandered through the crowd with tea and bowls of chips. Even Abby helped, bringing napkins and cups of ice to the guests. She looked happier than she had in a long time.

When Kate saw him enter with Lora, she smiled at him warmly—a smile he did not deserve, but she left him alone, too busy to spend time with any particular guest. Could it be she was uncertain and too polite to force conversation on a man who'd stalked out of her yard, twice?

At nine o'clock, he found himself alone with Kate between two groups of chattering, giggling girls. During that moment of privacy, he swallowed hard and forced out the words, "I'm working on it, Kate."

At first he didn't think she could hear him, with the babble of voices around them. She didn't react immediately, and he wasn't really sure he could repeat it as the groups began to dissolve and re-form, which placed the two adults in the center of the pandemonium. Quickly he added, "Please be patient."

Then she smiled, a sweet, loving expression, and she touched his hand for just a moment. "You know where to find me."

Before she could say more, Brooke grabbed her around the waist and said, "Aunt Kate, can we start serving the cake?"

She disappeared through the crowd and up to the porch while he watched. He felt a glimmer of joy and hope for the first time in a long, lonely time.

At ten, he took Lora home to bed. After he tucked her in, he kissed her.

He hadn't meant to do it, but while the party broke up across the alley, he stood in the backyard. His eyes were drawn to the shed where he'd locked up his cycle. He turned away, but his thoughts refused to budge.

It had been so long since he'd felt young and irresponsible, since he'd felt the wind rush past him and the excitement of taking a curve too fast, longing for the freedom of just him and the cycle on the open road. Back then, life had been full of endless possibilities.

He used to love riding the machine, the sound of the engine, the smell of gasoline, the vibration, the power. Why was it locked up when at this moment he wanted nothing more than to rev it up and take a quick ride?

He strode to the door of his mother's apartment and knocked. When she opened he said, "Mom, would you stay with Lora for a while? I want to take the hog out."

Was she going to cry? No, after an initial brightening of her eyes, she grinned. "I'm so glad. There's a gas can in the garage."

He nodded but before she could step past him toward the house to sit with Lora, he asked, "Do you know where my helmet and leather jacket are?"

She opened the hall closet and handed them to him. "I've been keeping them here for you." Then she handed him another helmet. "Just in case you think of someone who might want to go with you."

He gave it back. "Not yet, Mom. Not tonight, but maybe soon."

Yes, maybe soon.

Chapter Fifteen

Because it was a school night, all the guests had left by ten. Kate surveyed the yard and saw little mess to clean. Everyone had helped, picking up trash, washing dishes and carting off the borrowed chairs and tables.

After she put the now-cool grill in the shed, she started the last chore: shaking and folding the blankets. As she did, she replayed the scene with Rob in her mind, the short but interesting and perhaps promising few seconds they'd spent together. After much thought, she ended up with no more understanding of their relationship or lack of one than she'd had four hours earlier.

He said he was trying. That was good. She had to believe him, but the "Please be patient" line bothered her. Patience was not one of her virtues and Rob knew that very well. She'd always been a jump-in-now-and-pay-the-consequences-later woman. That quality had led to success in her career but, in the end, had destroyed it. She should have learned something from the experience, but, for the life of her, she didn't know what. It certainly wasn't patience.

"Do you need help, Aunt Kate?" Brooke stood in the kitchen door outlined by light from inside. "Mom was so tired, I sent her to bed."

Interesting twist in the mother-daughter dynamic: Brooke had sent her mother to bed.

"Everything's under control," Kate assured her.

Didn't she wish? At least cleaning the backyard was under control; whatever was going on between her and Rob, not nearly as much. She waved toward the house. "Go to sleep. I'll be in as soon as I get a few things taken care of."

When Brooke disappeared inside, Kate smoothed out the last wrinkle in the blankets, stacked them and headed toward the porch. A firefly flew past her on its erratic path. She smiled as its light flickered on and off.

Then she heard something.

What was that racket?

From the Chambers's driveway came a noise that sounded like an asthmatic cough until she realized it was the sputter of a motorcycle. Then the rider gave the engine more gas. The engine sputtered again then caught. After a few moments, she heard the bike head down the driveway.

The realization that Rob had started riding the bike again started Kate's emotions roiling with the force and power of that big engine.

Rob was riding the hog again. What did that mean? Both for him and for them?

Her heart soared at the possibilities suggested by Rob on his motorcycle. The conflicting emotions of joy and confusion made her ask herself if, after all the ups and downs they experienced in the past weeks, she still wanted something from Rob?

Well, of course she did or she wouldn't be standing here, her arms loaded with blankets and musing about the roar of the hog. If she didn't care about him, she wouldn't have attempted to catch a glimpse of him over the past few days and her heart wouldn't have jumped when he and Lora had entered the yard tonight.

She could easily fall in love—probably was well past that stage if she would admit it—with the Rob he had been, with the Rob he had become over the years, with the man he could be if he reached out to her. She refused to care for the Rob who still missed his wife so much he couldn't face life. She did not yearn for a damaged man who was content to live in his past and deny his grief.

"Oh, Rob, please hurry," she whispered. "I'm waiting."

She carried the blankets to the porch and opened the screen door with one hand. As she did, she heard the hog head down Goliad, its engine not firing on all cylinders but still moving along. She knew where he was going: down Highway 29 and east toward Burnet, a ride along the winding road where live oak trees and cedars arched above him, where white-tailed deer grazed along the road. The drive he'd always loved.

Maybe he'd take her someday.

Three days later, Kate sat in her office and scribbled edits on the page in front of her as she attempted to turn her mind away from three evenings of hearing Rob's cycle leave his driveway and three days of wondering what was going on. Was he working things out? Would he call her?

"Kate?" Lilibeth knocked and stuck her head through the door into Kate's office. "Someone delivered this thing for you."

The receptionist held out a basket of wild-flowers: golden sunflowers and shaggy pink basket flowers, bright yellow daisies mixed with red and yellow Texas lantana.

"Why would anyone send you a bunch of weeds?" She passed Kate the basket of flowers as if they were infected by a particularly virulent strain of the plague.

"They aren't weeds," Kate started to explain before she realized she'd never convince Lilibeth that what she held was more beauti-ful than a dozen roses because, she was sure, they came from Rob. She touched the vein of a sensitive briar and watched the leaves fold up.

"Here's this." Lilibeth gave her the envelope.

Kate pulled out the card. "Come for a ride with me tonight at eight?" she read to herself. "I'll bring a helmet for you." It was written in Rob's precise, square script.

Biting her lip, she closed her eyes and saw Rob's face, but not the cold, hard mask. This was the face of Rob as he'd watched her for only an instant after their second kiss, the few times he laughed and when joy had lighted his features, every one of them. This was the face of the Rob she wanted to share the rest of her life with. Opening her eyes, she ran her fingers over the words on the note until she had memorized them with her heart.

When she arrived home at four, Kate had to force her mind in other directions or the hours would drag by. She took the last load of blankets from the washer and shoved them in the dryer, she unloaded the dishwasher and put the clean dishes away and she swept off the porch and mopped both kitchens before she picked Abby up at work. When they entered the house, it was time to put dinner together.

"Rob's picking me up on his motorcycle tonight," Kate said after dinner as she picked up the plates and carried them to the sink.

"Oh, Aunt Kate, that's so cool. Do you think he'd take me for a ride sometime?"

"You'd have to ask him and your mother."

"Mom…"

But Abby didn't respond. Instead she stood and said in a flat voice, "Have a good time, Kate." She turned to leave the kitchen. "And thank you."

"For what?" For taking care of her? For

dinner? For being an absolutely magnificent sister?

"For folding the blankets and putting them away."

Well, that was a start. "You're welcome."

Once Abby had climbed the stairs to rest, Brooke said, "Are you going to marry Rob?"

For a moment, Kate continued to wipe the table. "I don't know." That was all the information she could give. "I just don't know."

"Well," Brooke said, her voice confident, "I think you'd be a great mother."

Oh, my. Marrying Rob did mean she'd be an instant mother. Was she ready for that? Brooke seemed to think so but, as usual, Kate hadn't considered every aspect and possible ramification of meeting Rob tonight. Like the one where she could end up being a mother.

Only an hour later, Kate sat on the front porch. Children rode their bicycles on the sidewalks. Across the street, Brooke played tag with a bunch of neighborhood kids, their laughter floating to where Kate waited.

At two minutes before eight, she heard the sound of the motorcycle starting in the Chambers's driveway. The first emotion she felt was fear, gripping her heart and making it beat wildly. As she drew in a deep breath and closed her eyes, she chastised herself. This was the most important evening she could remember. Of course she'd feel a little nervous.

But tonight she felt more than that. Tonight panic filled her precisely because this was such an important night. Then she heard the sound of the cycle turning the corner. She opened her eyes to see Rob, in his black leather jacket and brilliant red helmet as he turned the huge machine up the driveway. She felt the same joy the young Kate had felt when she watched him do the same so many years earlier.

He pulled the helmet off and smiled at her, lovingly, openly, completely, and her heart and breathing stopped. When finally her cardiac rhythm and respiration picked up to normal, she grinned back at him. Grabbing her denim jacket, she leaped down the steps and ran to where Rob sat on his shiny red hog. For a second, he put his hand on her arm, the smile never wavering.

Then he motioned toward the helmet he'd brought. "Put it on and let's go."

Quickly she tugged it on and tossed her leg over the seat. She settled in behind Rob and placed her hands around his waist, holding tightly.

"Ready?" At her consent, he revved the engine. "Listen to that power," he said. "I had to tune it up, but listen to it."

He turned the cycle and took off down the street. In minutes, they were out on the highway heading toward the lake, as they had done so often when they were young and in love and sure the world held everything they ever could want, as long as they were together.

As if he'd never quit riding, Rob took the curves cleanly, leaning into each while she held on. Combined with the speed of the ride and the closeness of Rob, she laughed, loud and long. Rob yelled something at her she couldn't hear, but she heard his laughter as she leaned her head against his back.

When he pulled up in the parking lot of the park, he steadied the machine and allowed her to get off before he pulled off his helmet and took hers. Eyes shining and grin wide, he said, "Was that the most fun you've ever had?"

She put her hand on his shoulder and nodded. "That was truly the most fun I've ever had." But only because she was with him. Otherwise the entire experience would have terrified her.

He stood, stowed the helmets and took off his jacket to drape it over the seat. "Come on."

He pulled her toward the lake and to the bench that overlooked the silver water, the bench that used to be their place. He sat and pulled her down next to him.

For a few minutes, they didn't talk, only watched the moon and its reflection and held hands.

"'O Lord, our Lord, how majestic is your name in all the earth! You have set your glory above the heavens,'" Rob whispered, quoting the Psalm. After a few more seconds, he said, "I came out for a few evenings to sit and watch the lake. I remembered those verses from the vesper service and thought and prayed."

She didn't say anything, just waited for him to continue.

"You know I loved Junie very much," he said, his eyes still on the sky.

Kate nodded.

"You know I loved you in high school and college." He gazed at her. "But Junie was my wife, the mother of our child. When she was diagnosed with cancer before Lora was born, it devastated me."

"Rob, I know. I'm sorry." She put her hand on his arm.

He lifted his eyes to the sky again and continued to speak. "I didn't know how to handle it." He clenched Kate's hand. "Exactly as you said, I didn't allow myself to grieve." He paused. "I denied the pain. I pretended to be strong so I could function, so I could get by. It didn't work." His voice broke. "A year and a half. It took eighteen months for the cancer to take her, and she fought until the end."

Kate leaned against him and kept her hand in his.

"I struggled so long with Junie's death. I looked for a reason for her suffering, any explanation, but couldn't find one. The platitudes people quoted didn't help. In the end, the only truth I could find was that Junie died. That was it." He shrugged and repeated, "She died."

He stopped talking for nearly a minute. "When she did, I couldn't find God anyplace." He gestured toward the sky. "What I've discovered over the past few days is that God is like the moon and the stars. God is the light in our darkness. God's always there, even on the darkest night. I realized if I can't find God, it's because I'm not looking. God's always there."

He looked at Kate, sad but almost relieved, then put his arm around her. "The problem was never with you, Kate. I was so angry with God for Junie's death."

"How could you be angry with God?" Kate struggled to understand his words.

"Sounds stupid, but I was. I've always been a good person. I thought if I prayed hard enough, Junie wouldn't die. But she suffered. The more she suffered, the more I thought prayer wasn't working, and the angrier I was with God. Why didn't He grant my prayers?" Then he whispered, "Why didn't He answer my prayers?"

Unable to answer the question, she clenched Rob's hand.

"Now I know that if I had listened, God was answering my prayers."

She continued to listen as she tried to follow his reasoning.

"I don't mean my prayer that Junie would recover and live, but my prayers for courage, my prayers that He'd always be with me." He looked at the sky. "God was beside Junie in her pain. God was with her and has always been with me."

"I had to find that out, too. God is always with us." Kate nodded. "Sometimes that's hard to see."

"It took a great deal of prayer to find this, and I've been talking with Reverend Moreno. He's helped a lot." He studied their hands for a moment. "Kate, now I want to go on with life."

"Oh, Rob, I'm so glad." She wanted to ask if there was a place for her in his life, but not yet. He wasn't finished, and she, well, she needed to be patient. At least for a few more minutes.

He pulled her against him and pressed a kiss on her tousled hair. "I don't know where that leaves us, you and me. I'm still learning and feel a little raw and uncertain."

"I understand."

"I can't promise anything now, Kate." He rubbed his cheek on her hair. "I still have a lot to work out, to learn to accept, but I want you to stay in Silver Lake. I want to see if we have a future together. Will you give me a chance? Will you give us a chance to be together?"

"Rob, I decided to stay here a week ago. Even if you and I couldn't work this out, I was going to stay. This is home."

"You already decided?" He leaned away from her, put his hand on her cheek and rubbed softly with his thumb. "You mean I've gone through this long explanation, and you've already decided to stay in Silver Lake?"

"I needed to hear it. You needed to tell me."

Rob nodded as he pulled her to her feet. His

eyes caressed her face for a moment before he kissed her, a sweet, loving kiss that promised a future even if he couldn't say the words yet.

For a moment, she snuggled against him before she pushed away to look up at his dear face. That's when she remembered Brooke's words. If she and Rob had a future together, she'd also have a daughter and a mother-in-law. She stepped back, away from his arms, and bit her lip.

"Okay, first, I need to tell you that I love you." When he would have stepped forward to gather her in his arms, she held up a hand. "Stop. Second, I need to ask you something." She cleared her throat. "Suppose… I mean, what if we do…oh, I don't know, get married someday, what will that mean, um, for your family?"

Rob leaned against a tree and watched her, not the least bit ill at ease. He didn't say a word, which made her feel really uncomfortable.

"How do you feel about that?" she asked.

"About what?" His lip quivered.

Was he laughing at her?

"Are you laughing at me?" she demanded.

He straightened. "Of course not."

In the brilliance of the moon shining on the

lake, she could see how serious his expression was, but she thought his lips were quivering.

"Okay," he admitted. "I'm enjoying this."

"What?" She blinked. "Why?"

"When we were in college, I kept trying to talk to you about getting married. You accepted my ring, you set a date, but you would never discuss it." He took a step toward her. "It's fun to watch you talking about it." Then he grinned. "Actually it's fun to hear you babbling about marriage."

Because she knew she had been babbling, Kate hurried to say, "I was and I shouldn't because you're not ready…"

"I'm not ready to get married, Kate, but I am ready and very willing to *talk* about the future, our future. Knowing you love me makes me feel a lot better about that future." He took her hand. "To answer your question, my mother would welcome you. She thinks you saved me."

"But Lora. How would she feel about a new mother, if, um, that were to happen?"

"Kate, she doesn't remember Junie at all. She's told me she'd really like to have a mother, like her friends and the other children at church."

"I know nothing about children." She bit her lip. "Would she accept me?"

"Of course. She already loves you. In fact, as I was leaving tonight, she suggested you'd make a good mommy, exactly the way you were Puppy's mommy."

"She did?"

He paused to study her face before he slowly said, "But here's the important question—how do you feel about having a daughter, a ready-made family?"

How did she feel? How could a woman not love to have a daughter like Lora? "Wonderful. She's a darling. Do you think…?"

"Kate, slow down." He took her hand. "Stop making plans. For now, let's concentrate on us."

"On us." The words made her ridiculously happy.

He looked down at her. "I love you." He folded her gently in his arms. "You love me. If we're together, the rest will come."

"If we're together, the rest will come," she repeated.

"First, let's celebrate the joy that God has brought us together, then I plan to kiss you and tell you how much I love you. Is that okay?"

"Oh, yes, that's very okay."

As they stood together, Kate was so filled with joy, she laughed. The sound bounced off the rippling reflection of the moon on Silver Lake and echoed back.

She was home. Here at the lake, here in Rob's arms, here in God's care, she was home. Finally home.

Epilogue

It was Easter Sunday, Kate's second since her return to Silver Lake. Because the morning had dawned dark and rainy, the sunrise service was held in the sanctuary. As they settled in the pew, Kate looked to her left where her husband sat with their four-year-old daughter on his lap.

They'd been married five months, five wonderful months. When they told Lora about their decision, she'd been so happy, she'd wanted to help plan the wedding. Her first suggestion had been to have several blond cocker spaniels as part of the wedding party. She was now satisfied with a black cocker she'd named, of course, Puppy.

Because the junior choir was leading the service, Brooke sat in the choir loft. Abby was there for the first time, to see her daughter. She sat to Rob's left, with his mother.

All around them were beloved friends and family. The only ones missing were the Watkinses, who were on a mission trip to Puerto Rico.

For Rob and Kate there was one more special reason to celebrate. She was having a baby. Could life become any better?

As the prelude started, Lora slid from her father's lap to Kate's and patted her on the stomach. "Our baby's in there," she announced to everyone sitting around them. Up until then, it had been a family secret. Well, no more.

Then the choir started singing "Hallelujah" and Kate listened again to the miracle of Easter morning.

This year, she had so many people to share it with. She was blessed. As she cuddled Lora on her lap and relaxed into Rob's arm around the back of the pew, she knew she'd never again, never again, take for granted the blessings she held so deep in her heart.

* * * * *

Dear Reader,

Many summers ago, I sat on the porch of a cabin in the Rocky Mountains, overwhelmed by the rugged beauty around me. Another summer I took part in a communion service in a boathouse surrounded by the water of Lake Michigan and was filled with peace.

Wherever we look, we are surrounded by God's creation: in the power of a thunderstorm, the brilliance of azaleas in Savannah, in the crashing of ocean waves against the shore. I've often found my faith strengthened in nature. I imagine you have, too.

For that reason, I set this story in the Texas Hill Country where I live surrounded by wildflowers and amazing beauty, a place where the moon shining on water can lead to deepening faith and love.

May nature remind us always of God's presence and the miracle of His love, for He has created a beautiful world for us to care for and enjoy.

Jane Myers Perrine

QUESTIONS FOR DISCUSSION

1. Has there been a special setting in nature—mountains, a lake—where you've been aware that God was close? Is it also possible to find God during a destructive act of nature such as a hurricane or flood?

2. Rob feels alone, unable to trust God because of the death of his wife. Where have you found strength during times of sorrow and crisis? Have you ever felt alone, as if God were missing in your life? What did you do?

3. Have you had a friend who has gone through a time when his or her faith was tested? Did you find a way to support this friend? How? How did he or she find their faith again?

4. Kate worked hard and succeeded in everything she tried until her integrity was tested. Has there been a moment in your life when you had to take a stand for something you believed? Have you ever faced a time when this stand cost you what you wanted most? How did you handle that?

5. Kate learned that she could succeed on her own, with her talent and her drive. However, she did this at the expense of relationships and sometimes hurt other people. Do you know others who aren't good in relationships or who ignore others in their drive to succeed? How could faith change those lives?

6. If we see problems in our friends' lives— broken personal relationships, addictions, depression—how can we speak a word of healing?

7. Rob discovers something he used to know: God never leaves us alone. God is always with us. It's we who turn our backs or don't see God's actions. Have you or someone you know ever gone through a time like this? How did you or your friend regain faith?

8. Determined to be strong, Rob doesn't allow others into his life. Why does he believe he has to be strong? Have you ever felt this way? Did it help you or hurt you?

9. Have others you are close to shut you out during their times of pain? How did you feel? Were you able to reach that person?

10. Kate refuses to build a relationship with a man who is still mourning his wife. Do you agree with her decision? When she confronts Rob with her fear that he hasn't grieved for his wife, do you agree with her action? Why or why not?

11. Kate now regrets that she hurt her sister and didn't come home to see her parents. She has a hard time forgiving herself for this. How can we find forgiveness for our mistakes? How can we help others?

12. When Kate heard the sound of Rob's motorcycle, she was thrilled. Why? Have you seen action in either your own life or other people's lives that show they are changing, able to accept love and life again?

Love Inspired®

SUSPENSE

RIVETING INSPIRATIONAL ROMANCE

Watch for our new series of
edge-of-your-seat suspense novels.
These contemporary tales
of intrigue and romance
feature Christian characters
facing challenges to their faith...
and their lives!

Steeple
Hill®

Visit:
www.SteepleHill.com